FALLING
OUT OF PLACE

M.G. Higgins

SADDLEBACK
EDUCATIONAL PUBLISHING

GRAVEL ROAD

SADDLEBACK
EDUCATIONAL PUBLISHING
www.sdlback.com

ISBN-13: 978-1-62250-021-5
ISBN-10: 1-62250-021-0
eBook: 978-1-61247-664-3

Printed in Guangzhou, China
NOR/0716/CA21601269

20 19 18 17 16   4 5 6 7 8

Gravel Road

CHAPTER

1

My parents are lame. I mean, really lame. Right now they're in the living room talking about me. Dad likes to rant in Spanish. I hear him flick something with his finger. Probably my C-average report card.

I'm sitting on my bed with my knees drawn up to my chest. I pick at a loose thread on the hem of my LA Sparks T-shirt. I have to wait for my parents to finish talking. That's the rule. I don't get a say. After they decide my fate, they'll let me know. I'm guessing it will be no TV and no dating Tony for a month. That's my usual punishment. Tony will understand if we can't go out. He's as loyal as a puppy dog. I don't care, as long as I can play basketball.

I push a deep breath out of my chest. I really should get some homework done. I lean over and yank my backpack off the floor. I'm not even sure what homework I have. A literature essay, I think. Except I haven't read the book we're supposed to write about. A research paper for my government class. There's a test in geometry tomorrow. Or is it Friday?

I unzip my backpack. The inside looks like my locker threw up in it. My stomach twists with stress. I lean my head against the wall and think about texting Tony. Maybe let him know what's up. But my hands feel like lead and fall onto my lap. I stretch my legs out.

Across the room, my *quinceañera* portrait stares back at me. I look like the queen of unicorns in my white ball gown and sparkly crown. Talk about lame. I can't believe I agreed to that big church service when I turned fifteen. Or the huge party. It cost my parents a bundle, as much as Celia's party. Dad has never said so, but I know he's pissed he had four daughters.

From the living room I hear him bark, "*Y no mas baloncesto!*"

What? My face gets hot. The leaden feeling vanishes. I jump off my bed and run into the living room. Mom and Dad are facing each other, their arms crossed. I see Rosie and Marta at the kitchen table. Their school books are open, but I can tell they're listening.

I glare at Dad. "What do you mean 'no more basketball'?"

He glares back at me. I expect him to order me to my

room. But he says, "When Celia was seventeen, she had a job and got straight As."

"So?" I cross my arms, copying them.

"So there's an opening in the warehouse," Mom says. "Two hours after school and all day Saturday."

"I don't spend that much time playing basketball!" I shout.

"No TV or dates for a month." It's as if Dad didn't hear me. "And no cell phone."

"What? No!" My phone is a cheap piece of crap. But it's my lifeline. I scramble for an excuse. "What if I have an emergency?"

"If you're not home, you'll be at school or work. Those places have phones," Dad says. He pauses. "We expect you to raise every one of your grades. By the end of the semester. Or no cell phone until you graduate."

I stare at him with my mouth open. "There's no way! I'm not as smart as Celia. I can't raise all of my grades. Especially geometry."

"You can. You're choosing not to." Of course that's what Dad says. He moved here from Mexico with nothing. He works hard. So does Mom. My older sister, Celia, is just like them. She's in college on a scholarship. The three of them think anything is possible if you just try hard enough. Well, I have tried. It's not possible.

"Screw you," I tell him.

"Gabriella!" Dad yells.

Mom gasps. "Respect your father!"

I march back to my room. Slam the door. Wish it had a lock. I think about sneaking out. Hooking up with Tony. But I'm already in enough trouble. Grabbing my phone off my desk, I start to call Uncle Mike. He'll understand when I tell him what a jerk his big brother is being.

The door flies open just as I'm pressing his number. Dad steps into my room and holds out his palm. I press my lips together, grip my phone. He doesn't say anything. Just stares. I loosen my grip. Drop it onto his hand.

His eyes soften a little. "We only want what's best for you, Gabby." He glances at my photo over the dresser. Then he says, "You're not a child any more." He leaves, closing the door behind him.

My bed feels cold and clammy when I crawl into it. I curl into a ball. My friend Randi tells me I'm lucky I have two parents. I'm lucky they're married and not divorced. I'm lucky my dad's not in prison. Or drunk. Or having kids with other women.

Yeah. Lucky me.

CHAPTER

2

Randi's short Afro is the first thing I see when I walk into school the next morning. She's standing in front of her locker. At six feet, she towers over most other students. She looks way more like a basketball player than I do at only five eight.

"Hey," I mutter, stepping up behind her.

She twists around. "Hey, Gabs." She slams her locker shut. "What's wrong?"

"What do you mean?"

"You didn't return my texts last night," she said.

"Oh. Right." We make our way down the crammed hallway to first period. "I had a big fight with my parents. Dad took my phone until I raise every grade."

Randi's eyes widen in horror. "No way! Even geometry?"

I nod.

"Wow. Severe." She's quiet a few seconds. Then she shrugs. "At least they care. Mom barely glanced at my report card last night."

At least. I hate those words. Being turned into a clone of my sister doesn't feel like my parents care very much. But I don't want to explain all of that again. "So what were you texting me about that was so freakin' urgent?"

We've reached her English class. "Um," she mumbles without looking at me. "Nothing important." She's frowning. "I've got make-up chem lab at lunch. See you at basketball."

Randi walks into her classroom.

Okay, so my frustration leaked out. I got a little snarky. Randi is so sensitive. I reach into my backpack for my phone. I'll text her with a simple *sorry*. But I can't find my phone! Then I remember.

Crap.

I shift my backpack on my shoulder and trudge to social studies.

I tend to block things out of my head that I don't want to think about. That's why I didn't mention to Randi that my parents expect me to quit basketball and get a job. It's also why I go to the gym after school. Somewhere in my brain, I hope Mom and Dad have changed their minds. A bigger part of my brain knows they haven't. But at the moment, my ignoring brain cells are in full control.

We're warming up, on our first lap around the court. Running laps isn't my favorite activity in the world, but it beats working at a friggin' job. Randi is up ahead. She ignored me in the locker room when we were suiting up. I take a deep breath. It's time to get us back to normal. I sprint and catch up.

"Hey," I say, struggling to stay even with her long strides.

"Hey." Her voice is all mopey.

I take a deep breath. "So how's it going with El Paco?"

That gets a small smile out of her. She shrugs.

"Is that what you were texting me about?" I ask.

She nods. "He's being a jerk." Randi then describes the fight she had with her boyfriend, Franklin Jamison. He lives in the Valley. They met last year at a basketball tournament. It's a long-distance romance. He complains about spending money on gas. She's constantly jealous. As usual, she's worried he's dating another girl. He backed out of their weekend plans.

She finally finishes her sob story. Before I can tell my mouth to stop, I spit out, "Dump him."

She slows to a walk and stares at me. "What?"

She wanted me to tell her not to worry. That he loves her. That they're the perfect couple. Except … I'm not in the mood.

"Well yeah," I say. "It's clearly not working out. You only talk about how miserable you guys are."

"But I like Franklin. I don't want to break up." Her toffee-colored skin can't hide the angry red darkening her cheeks. "Gabby," she sputters, "you can be so—"

From center court, Coach Matthews shouts, "Line up! Shooting drills!"

We join our teammates behind the free-throw line. Randi's arms are crossed. She looks away from me.

I complete the sentence she started a minute ago. I can be so insensitive. So bitchy. Whatever. It was just my opinion. Randi has been high maintenance since we met freshman year. I'm tired of apologizing for myself. I'm tired of always having to fix what I say.

I feel hyped up all of a sudden. I really need to play. I bounce up and down on my toes. Everyone. Is. Moving. So. Slowly. "Come on!" I clap my hands. "Let's go!" I practically tear the ball from Tiana for my free throw.

"Hey," she whines.

"What?" I dribble the ball a few times, bashing it on the floor. I lift the ball, eye the basket, and throw. It misses wide. "Crap."

I race up, grab the rebound, and toss it into the basket.

"Gabby," Coach says. "What are you doing?" Getting our own rebounds is not part of the drill.

"Sorry. I got carried away."

By the time the game starts, I want to play so bad I can scream. My best friend doesn't understand me. My parents don't understand me. But basketball? We are simpatico.

I play small forward. That's position number three. It means I do a little of everything on the court. Foul shooting is my specialty. I make about sixty-five percent of every free throw I try. That's pretty good. In order to shoot fouls, I have to draw fouls. That's easy because I'm aggressive. I get to the line quick on layups and post-up plays. In the process I'm always running smack into defenders.

My muscles are twitching when our opponents trot onto the court. The St. Barnard Tigers. They're a Catholic high school, like us. We're the All Saints Crusaders. It's amazing how ruthless our teams play each other. I figure God must like winning games more than he likes people sitting around reading the Bible. I'm up for that. Yay, God.

Once the game starts, everything else melts away. It's just me, sprinting, watching the ball, passing the ball, dribbling the ball, shooting the ball. If people in the stands are yelling, I don't hear them. Coach gets on my case for not listening to instructions from the sidelines. I can't help it. I'm too focused on the court.

Alicia has just nabbed a missed rebound on the Tiger's side of the court.

I'm open. "Here!" I yell.

She passes to me. I surge toward the three-point line. The Tiger's point guard steps in front of me. She's tall and hefty. She reaches out to steal the ball. I run straight through her tree-limb arms, trying to draw a foul.

Instead, we get tangled up. I trip over her big feet. The wooden floor rises up and slaps my right cheek. *Smack*. The rest of my body follows.

For a second, I lie on my stomach, dazed. The court swims around me. Something snaps. She tripped me. The bitch tripped me. My blood turns hot.

I push myself onto my hands, searching for her. Randi is gripping my arm. She helps me stagger to my feet. There's a worried crease between her eyebrows. She's asking me something. I don't hear her. I don't hear anything except an annoying buzz.

There she is. Standing with her teammates under the basket. She's wearing a satisfied smirk. At least, that's what it looks like to me. My skin, my muscles, everything is on fire. I shake Randi's hands off my arm. I take four steps, and I'm fighting with a Tiger.

Jamala and I are grappling on the floor. That's her name. I know because I hear her teammates saying it over and over. That must mean my ears are working again. I'm swinging punches. Most of them don't connect, but a couple do. She's yanking my hair and scratching me with her fingernails. I keep thinking it should hurt, but I don't feel anything. Just the scorching blood pounding through me.

Coach yells, "Gabby! Stop! Gabby!"

A ref's whistle blows.

Girls scream.

People are grabbing me by the shoulders and arms and pulling me to my feet. I'm breathing hard. Someone's helping Jamala get upright. With a zing of satisfaction, I see her lip is bleeding. A lump is forming under her left eye.

"Crazy bitch!" she screams. She glares death rays at me before her coach and teammates lead her to their bench.

"What were you thinking?" Coach is in my face. "Wipe off that smile. You look like an animal."

I don't care. I feel like an animal. But I take a deep breath and at least try to match Coach's frown.

She shakes her head. Walks away and joins the ref. The ref keeps pointing at me. I can't hear what she says, but it can't be good.

I'm starting to feel my cheek where I fell. It hurts. My arms sting. I look at them. They're covered with scratches. Some are bleeding. I notice a chunk of hair on the floor. Gross. I touch the tender spot on my head where it came from. I take another deep breath.

"What happened?" It's Randi, the crease still between her eyes.

"I don't know," I answer. It's the truth. Mostly. I wanted to get back at that girl. But I guess I didn't mean to go ballistic.

Randi looks at my hair on the floor. Then she meets my eyes. "There's something wrong, Gabby."

"I know!" I glance at the ref and Coach again. "I got tripped. Now they're blaming me."

Randi takes a deep breath. "No, I mean …." She pauses again. "There's something wrong with you. You need help, or something."

I stare at her. What is she talking about?

"You're pissed off all the time," she says. Then her voice is so soft I barely hear her. "You scare me. Just a little. But you scare me." With that, my best friend turns and walks to the bench.

I just stand there. Only a chunk of my hair for company. Now that the adrenalin has worn off, I feel shaky. Drained. Stupid. Embarrassed. And cold. I rub my arms. I watch Randi slump onto the bench. Alicia sits next to her. If Randi's scared of me, that's her problem, not mine. I don't need help. She does. I send her comment where it belongs. To the room in my brain that hides things I don't want to think about.

"Gabby." Coach motions me to the sidelines. I follow her. At the locker-room doorway, she stops and turns. "You're suspended from the game."

It's what I expected, so I don't argue.

She looks at my arms. The scratches aren't that bad. It's not like blood is dripping on the floor or anything.

"Make sure you wash those in the shower with soap and warm water," she says. "Use some antibacterial salve when you get home. Okay?"

I nod.

"Do you feel all right? Do you want me to call your parents?"

"No."

She takes a deep breath. "Gabby, you've had too many serious infractions this season. This is your last warning. I'll have to drop you from the team if you lose your temper again."

I shrug and open the locker-room door.

"You're a terrific player," Coach says. "Colleges will be competing to recruit you. But you've got to calm down."

I hate her lectures. They're so boring. I start to walk into the locker room. Then I grab the door and twist around. "Hey, Coach."

She looks at me.

"I quit."

"What?"

"Yeah. I quit." I tap the door.

Coach sighs. "You're being impulsive, Gabby. Think about it first."

"I don't need to. Anyway, it's what my parents want."

Five minutes later I'm standing in the shower. I've got the water turned on as hot and as hard as I can stand it. I press my forehead against the tile wall. Tiny bullets of lava water rip against my back. The part of my brain that thought Mom and Dad might let me keep playing basketball? I knew better. Once they make up their minds about something, it sticks. Always. I knew that. I really did. So that was my last game. I knew it was my last game before it started.

I like how my tears mix with the shower water so I don't have to see them.

"Where have you been?" Mom asks. I've just walked into the house. I've barely closed the door behind me.

"Basketball." I meet her gaze and slide my backpack off my shoulders.

"Gabriella! We told you—" Her mouth forms a shocked *O* when she sees my arms. "What happened?"

"A fight. No big deal."

"A fight?"

"Yeah. Do we have any antibacterial stuff?"

I follow her to the bathroom. I sit on the closed toilet seat. She fixes me up while scolding me for disobeying them. And for fighting. Then she tells me about my interview at Grocery Mart where she clerks. She's worked it all out. I'll be meeting with Jake the warehouse manager tomorrow. Right after school. I should wear a blouse with long sleeves to hide my arms. And makeup to cover my cheek that's now turning purple. First impressions are important, she tells me.

I nod solemnly. I'm on it, Mom. I am, like, totally excited to begin this new chapter of my life. Because I'm all grown up and responsible now. Basketball is for slackers. Everyone knows that.

CHAPTER

4

The Grocery Mart warehouse entrance is at the corner far-
thest from the main store. A brick props the door open. I
walk in. The scent of ripe bananas and wet cardboard hit
me. The building is about the size of our school gym. Mom
told me it's also a distribution center for other LA stores.
That's why it's so big.

Beep-beep-beep.

There's a yellow pallet-lifting thingy backing up at the
other end of the building. A forklift. After it reverses, it
charges forward, vanishing behind an impossibly tall shelf.
Haven't these people heard of earthquakes?

"Gabriella?"

I turn. "Um, yeah. Yes. Gabby."

"Gabby. Great. I'm Jake Matthews. Warehouse
manager."

He sticks his hand out. I shake it. The guy is white, middle aged, a little paunchy. His scraggly mustache reminds me of the weeds growing in the cracks of our driveway. He's wearing a grimy LA Dodgers baseball cap.

He lets go of my hand. Returning to the door, he flicks the brick out of the doorway with a practiced kick. It slams shut. Now there's no sunlight. Just the glow of the overhead fluorescents. I notice the ceiling is made of metal. I wonder what it sounds like in the rain.

"You're on time. That's good." He motions me toward a room against the wall. "Your mom said you're very responsible."

Right. I nod like this is something I hear all the time. I step inside the room, which must be an office. Glass windows look out onto the warehouse. It's got file cabinets and a desk. And paper. Lots of paper.

"Have a seat," he says.

I would, except they're covered with paper. I just stand there.

"Oh," he says. He grabs the pile off one chair. Then he adds it to the pile on the chair next to it. "Sorry."

I sit and grip the armrests.

"So," he says, plopping into the swivel chair behind his desk. It squeaks. Makes me think of a screaming mouse. He reaches into the middle of a stack of paper and magically pulls out a single sheet. He glances at it. "I see on your application you've never had a paying job before."

Huh? What application? Since I don't remember filling one out. Then I figure Mom or Dad must have done it. Like my printing isn't neat enough or something. "Um, yeah." Then I add, "But I've been babysitting my younger sisters forever."

He nods, still looking at the application. "I see that." He glances at me and grins. "Kids can be a handful. I've got three."

I nod. It's hot in here. Sweat drips under my long-sleeved shirt.

"You have to be physically fit for warehouse work. But with your background in basketball, I'm guessing that won't be a problem."

I nod again. Is my entire life story on that thing?

He raises an eyebrow. "Can you lift forty pounds?"

I shrug, not a clue. "Sure."

He sets down the application and looks at me. "In an ideal world, I'd only hire ex-linebackers for this job. It's heavy, dirty work. But my biggest problem is lack of responsibility. I need people here on time, every shift, ready to work." He points at the pile of papers on the chair next to mine. "Most of those are termination documents and unemployment claims."

He clears his throat. "Look, Gabby. I know your mom. She's a good person. A hard worker. She says you're a hard worker. I'm going to take her word for it." He smiles. "Plus, she said she'll kill you if you mess up."

I dig my fingernails into the armrests.

"So, I suppose you want the job or you wouldn't be sitting here."

I pause a second. "Yeah. Yes."

He reaches his hand across the desk. "Welcome to Grocery Mart."

What? That's it? I shake his hand. "Okay. Thanks."

He settles back into his chair. The mouse screams again. "Paperwork, rules, and then tour."

The forms I fill out are long. The list of rules takes longer than my interview. He gives me handouts on how to lift. With your knees, not your back. Okay. No open-toed shoes. So sandals are out. How to make an injury report. How to send my paycheck directly to my bank account. Except, I don't have a bank account.

Then Jake (that's what he says I should call him) leaves to find someone to give me a tour. I slump into my chair and tap the armrests. My feelings are all over the place. I'm a little overwhelmed. Panicky. Like this is happening too fast. I'm sad I'm not at basketball practice. There's a huge tournament Saturday I don't want to miss.

I'm still mad at my parents for forcing me into this job. And they filled out the application. What was up with that?

But, to be honest, I'm also a little excited. I'll be making my own money. Not an allowance Dad doles out when he feels like it. Money I've earned. That feels good. It put a smile on my face at school today when I thought about it. It's the reason I acted polite and answered all of Jake's questions. If I can't play basketball, then making money is an okay Plan B. It will help me make my escape when I turn eighteen.

"Gabby?"

I twist in my chair and look up. Jake is standing in the doorway. Looming behind him is a guy with raven-black hair and tawny skin. His features are sharp and angular. It's hard to tell what nationality he is. He could be half the population of LA. He's frowning and staring absently into Jake's office. It's like he'd rather be anywhere than here. Two words come to mind: bored and cocky.

"This is Evan," Jake says.

Behind Jake's back, Evan sticks out his long tongue. He pretends to lick Jake's ear.

Hah! I bite my lip to keep from cracking up.

Jake twists around and glares at Evan.

Evan's bored look is back in an instant. He stares at Jake, wide-eyed. "What?"

Jake shakes his head and says to me, "Evan will show you around."

"Okay," I mutter, trying to keep my smile in check. "Thanks." I get up and follow Evan out of Jake's office. Who is this guy?

CHAPTER

5

Evan looks over his shoulder after we leave Jake's office. "Dickwad," he mutters.

I wait for him to explain his opinion of my new boss. But he suddenly stops walking and I almost bump into him. We're back near the staff entrance. He points down the closest row of shelves. It seems to stretch forever.

"This is row *F*, your basic paper products. Towels, Kleenex, TP." He glances at the pile of handouts I'm holding. "Jake gave you a map of the warehouse, right?"

I rummage through them and shake my head.

"No map, but he gave you a direct-deposit form. Like we don't cash our paychecks the second we get them." He sighs. "Well, the layout isn't rocket science. Six rows, *A* through *F*. The rotting stuff is kept in the cooler, near the store." He points to the wall opposite where we're standing. I see wide double doors with rubber around the edges.

"Row *A* is pastries and bread," he continues. "*B* is crackers and chips. And so on. Aisles two and three run between the middle rows. Aisles one and four go around the outside. You'll figure it out fast enough." He looks at me. "Any questions?" His eyes sparkle a little, like this is all a big joke.

"Well, um, yeah. What do I do, exactly?"

He snorts. "Jake didn't explain that, either? Idiot." Then he rattles off, "You open crates. Move stuff into the store. Stock shelves. Do inventory. Oh, and when you hear, 'Cleanup on aisle whatever.' That's you. You're cleanup."

"So, are you also a …?" I pause. "I guess I don't know what my title is."

Slowly, like he's talking to two-year-old, he says, "You're a warehouse helper. I'm a material handler."

My cheeks warm. "I'm not usually this clueless. My mom set this up. She clerks in the store. Yolanda Herrera?"

"Oh yeah, Yolanda. Nice lady. I see the family resemblance."

"You do?"

He squints and gives me a crooked smile. "No. Not really."

Suddenly, Evan is reaching into his pocket and pulling out his vibrating phone. He grins as he reads the screen. "Jo wants to know if the new guy is an ox, a moron, or an oxymoron." He punches the keypad.

Somewhere in the middle of the warehouse, I hear a loud *beep-beep-beep-beep-beep*. Then the yellow forklift is speeding down the aisle right for us. I back up, afraid the metal lifters will chop me off at the knees. The machine stops a few inches from Evan. He doesn't flinch.

"Liar," the driver yells down at him.

Evan shrugs. "Gabby, meet Jo. Jo, meet Gabby."

Jo, a girl, jumps to the cement floor. She's wearing five earrings in each ear. I count them. They're all hoops with the smallest at the top and the biggest at the bottom. Her straight, dark brown hair is tucked behind her ears. "You don't look a thing like Chris Hemsworth," she informs me.

Evan grins sheepishly.

"Whatever," Jo says. "Welcome to the it-beats-flipping-burgers-at-McDonald's warehouse."

"Thanks," I say. I point at the forklift. "Do I get to drive that thing?"

"Big Bird?" She pats it. "Sure. The next time it snows on City Hall." Then she says, "You need special training."

Jo climbs back onto Big Bird. It beeps a few times and she takes off.

I finish the official tour with Evan. I find out that he and Jo are good friends. They hang out together after work. If I start my shift on time and don't leave early, Jake and I will get along just fine. I shouldn't wear "pretty" shirts like the one I've got on today. And Evan is looking forward to working with me. And he's got one of the most lopsided smiles I've ever seen. It can't tell if it's sneaky or … cute.

I think about the interview as I walk home from the bus stop. It wasn't that bad. Evan and Jo seem okay. Better than working with old people I have nothing in common with. Even so, by the time I get to the sidewalk outside our house, I'm feeling grumpy. It's one of those strange LA winter days that's close to ninety. I'm sweating like crazy. My feet hurt. The high of landing my first job is starting to wear off. I'm going to be at that warehouse five afternoons a week. All day Saturday. No basketball. It's feeling like a prison sentence already.

When I turn down our walkway, I see Tony. He's sitting on the top step in front of my house. He gives me a two-fingered wave. It may be the heat, but I'm not all that happy to see him.

I lower myself to the cement step. Leave several inches of air space between us. Thankfully, we're covered in late-afternoon shade. I grab the front of my shirt. Billow it in and out, blowing on my skin.

"Can I do that?" Tony asks.

It's so lame, I don't respond. Not even a smile.

He stretches his legs out. Leans back on his hands and sighs. "So, Yolanda and Raul took your phone?"

I nod, still blowing on my chest. He's always called

my parents by their first names. Our families are friends. I start to get dizzy from the blowing and stop. I lean back on my hands. Our little fingers touch.

"You could have come over and told me," he says. "I left you like a hundred messages. I thought you were really mad at me or something."

"I'm not mad. I've had a lot on my mind."

"Like what?"

I shrug my shoulders.

He shakes his head.

"What?" I ask.

"You used to talk to me about stuff."

I think about it. He's right. Since I was eight and we moved here from our old apartment. I've always shared my problems with Tony. I'm not sure when things changed. They just did. Now … I don't know. It's confusing. The fact that we go to different schools—him to public, me to parochial—doesn't help. "Sorry," I tell him. "I should have told you about the phone."

He kisses my cheek and gets to his feet. "What about Saturday? A movie?"

"Can't, I'm grounded. Anyway, I've got a job now."

"Oh, right." His voice is tight. "Raul told me about your interview. So you got it?"

I guess he's upset he heard about my job from Dad and not from me. "Yeah."

"Cool. Way to go." He hops down the steps. "We'll hang out here Saturday."

"I don't know. I'll have to ask."

He flashes a hopeful smile and the same two-finger wave. Then he jumps over the hedge and disappears.

I take a deep breath. Get to my feet. I face the house, preparing to deal with my dad. He's going to grill me about why I didn't tell Tony about losing my phone and being grounded. Then Dad is going to remind me how smart and polite Tony is. That he's not a gangbanger. That he's going places. That he's the best boyfriend I could ever hope for.

And yet, here I am, flipping my middle finger at my future. "What's wrong with you?" Dad will ask, his face all red. "I don't know!" I'll answer, throwing my hands in the air. Whether he believes me or not, it will be the truth.

CHAPTER

6

It's Friday morning. The first day of my new job. (Who starts a new job on a Friday?) It's also two days after my rampage in the gym. I laid low at school yesterday, keeping to myself. That wasn't hard, since my teammates avoided me too. It's always like this when I lose my temper at a game. Mutual embarrassment. It lasts a day, then it's over, like it never happened.

This morning I'm dying to talk to Randi. She doesn't know about my new job. I want to tell her about Evan and Jo and my dickwad boss. I want to know how practice went yesterday. I want to find out who Coach is replacing me with. Hopefully Tiana. She's my backup and deserves the position. If so, I want to give her some advice for tomorrow's tournament.

From down the hallway, I see Randi at her locker. I squeeze through the crowd. But when I'm close enough to call her name, she's gone. Her head bobs toward her English class. She's walking with someone. Alicia, I think. Okay. No biggie. I'll catch her at lunch.

We're not the biggest school in LA by far. Even so, Randi and I don't share any classes this semester. The morning drags. At lunch, the cafeteria line is long. By the time I grab a slice of pizza and an orange, it's late. I'm sure Randi is already at our table. She always brings a sandwich from home.

But two guys are sitting there. No Randi. I stand near the checkout counter and look quickly around. I hear familiar laughter and search for it. She's sitting near the back. Across from Alicia. A bunch of other team members are there too. Which makes sense, since it's the table where the team sits.

I grip my tray. A while back, Randi and I decided to find our own table. It's not that I don't like those girls, it's just … I take a deep breath and head down the aisle. The bench is crowded. Randi is sitting on the end.

"Hey." I slide my tray halfway onto the table. It bumps her apple.

She looks at me, hesitates, and scoots over.

I sit next to her. "What's up?"

She shrugs, staring at her sandwich. Everyone's quiet, focused on their food. Whatever they were laughing at earlier, I guess it isn't funny anymore.

"I got a job," I tell Randi.

She chews and swallows. "Cool." Her voice is flat.

Okay. She's upset. Why? It's been over a day since the game. I wrack my brain. Well, whatever has her panties in a knot, it's up to me to fix it, as always. I smile. "How did practice go yesterday?"

"Pretty good," Randi mutters.

"It went great," Alicia chirps. "Coach has Tiana playing third position. She's awesome. You should have seen all the three-pointers she laid up."

Tiana, who's sitting next to Alicia, squirms. "I wasn't that good. Not as good as Gabby."

"Just about," says Celeste. Then she mumbles, "At least you didn't hit anybody."

The table goes quiet again. My stomach tightens.

Finally, Tiana glances at me. "I'm sorry about … Well, it's not how I wanted to become a starter."

I don't know what to say. That it's not how I wanted her to become a starter, either? That I wish my parents didn't give a crap about my grades? I take a bite of pizza, just for something to do. It tastes like cardboard. I toss the slice back on my plate.

Alicia says to Randi, "We're gonna rock that tournament tomorrow. Your rebounding was hot yesterday."

Randi says, "Yeah, things kind of clicked at practice."

Then they're all talking about the practice I didn't go to.

And about the big tournament I won't be playing in. Part of me is relieved they aren't paying attention to me any more. But then I notice something. Randi is all chatty. A lot more than she usually is with me. And she's laughing. Smiling. She says Franklin will be at the tournament. She can't wait to see him.

That's when I remember. On Wednesday before the game, I told Randi to dump the love of her life. And I remember something else. After the fight, she told me I'm pissed off all the time. That I scare her. *I scare her.*

At this very moment she's leaning away from me. Her elbow juts toward me like a defensive block. I connect her body language to what she told me at the game. My stomach turns.

I can't fix us anymore. I can't fix us because we're no longer friends. That's what she's telling me without telling me.

Heat spreads from my chest up into my face. Out to my fingers. My jaw clenches. My muscles twitch. I shove my tray across the table. It slams into Alicia's water bottle, which launches into her lap. She shrieks. The orange flies off my tray. Bounces across the table. Rolls onto the floor. Not only is the table silent, so is half the lunchroom.

I get to my feet. Slam the door open with my fists. Storm out.

CHAPTER

7

I never, ever thought I'd look forward to going to a job. That's how bad my crappy day is going. I take the city bus from school to Grocery Mart. No transfers, so it doesn't take long. Mom's shift ends the same time as mine, five o'clock. She'll give me a ride home. Fun. She'll ask me lots of questions. I won't answer them.

As I walk across the Grocery Mart parking lot, I've got butterflies in my stomach. I have no idea what to expect. Or how much of an idiot I'll make of myself. From here I can see the staff entrance is closed. No brick props the door open like before. I try the knob. It's locked. I press the buzzer. I press it again. And again. It feels like I stand there for a year before someone finally opens it.

"What?" It's a big, older guy I've never seen before. He's got long graying hair pulled back in a ponytail. A tattoo of a snake coils up his neck.

"Um … I work here," I tell him.

He grunts and pulls the door open wider. I step inside.

"What's your name?" he asks.

"Gabby."

"Hutch," he grumbles. The door slams shut.

I look toward the office. I can see through the windows that the lights are off.

"Jake's gone home for the day," Hutch says, guessing my question. "He told me there was a new employee starting. I'm supposed to show you the ropes." Then under his breath he adds, "I really wish he'd stop hiring little girls."

Um … okay. "Are Evan and Jo here?"

"No."

"Oh. Since they were here yesterday, I just figured …"

He reaches into his pocket and pulls out something metal. It's the length of his palm. He slides a lever on top with his thumb. A razor blade juts out.

I step back.

He snickers. "Relax. Never seen a utility knife before?"

"Yes," I lie. Will I always feel like an idiot here?

Hutch turns and walks away. After a few steps, he glances over his shoulder. "Well, come on. I can't train you long distance."

What an asshole. I take a deep breath and catch up with him.

Breaking down cardboard boxes is not exciting. But it's

easy to learn. Once Hutch sees I've got the hang of it, he leaves me alone. After an hour kneeling on concrete, my knees hurt. I guess I imagined my first day of work would be a little different. Like I'd get to ride on the forklift. And trade insults with Evan and Jo. This is so not fun. I lean back on my heels. My fingers hurt. I flex them.

"Where are you kneepads?" a familiar voice asks.

I look up. Mom shakes her head. "Hutch," she says in disgust. She marches off.

Two minutes later, she returns with a set of rubber thingies with Velcro straps. She drops them on the floor next to me. "Put these on." She crosses her arms. "Jake's going to hear about this."

"What? No. Don't get him into trouble."

She's frowning, her lips pressed together. "You're entitled to—"

"Mom, please. Do you want them to think I'm a troublemaker?"

This gets her attention. Her features soften. She shakes her head. "There's a list of OSHA rules posted outside Jake's office. Read them. Ask for the safety equipment you need."

"Fine." I don't know what *osha* is. I don't care. Mom needs to make up her mind. Am I old enough to hold a job? Or am I a little girl she needs to take care of? "So are you back here checking up on me?"

"I'm just seeing how you're doing. Meet me in the parking lot when you get off at five. Remember, Abuelita's for dinner."

Oh, right. Grandma's. I'd almost forgotten.

"Well," Mom says. She gives me a small smile. "Work hard, Gabriella."

"What does it look like I'm doing?" I know I'm being rude. This day has just completely sucked. She opens her mouth like she's about to scold me. But she turns and walks back to the store.

I've just strapped on the kneepads when the loud-speaker shrieks, "Cleanup on aisle five!"

"Hey, girlie!" I hear from somewhere in the warehouse. "That's you!"

I sigh. Rip off the pads and drop them to the floor. Unless it's puke, a trip inside the store sounds better than cutting boxes. I get to the end of aisle five. Look at the mess in the middle of the floor. Just my luck, it's puke. But when I get closer, I see it's a broken jar of applesauce.

We eat dinner at Grandma's house one Friday every month. She's my dad's mom. Dad's the oldest of four brothers. They're all married and have kids except for Mike, the youngest. He's twenty-three and my favorite uncle. We have a lot in common. Like being picked on by my dad.

The table is crowded with aunts and uncles and the two girl cousins who've had their *quinceañera*—me and Teresa. She's sixteen and still into boy bands. Probably a virgin. We have nothing in common and hardly ever talk. The little cousins race around the house, screaming. I glance at Mike across the table. We roll our eyes at the same time.

Uncle Mike is gay. I think I'm the only person in the family who knows. A year ago he went to one of my basketball games. Afterwards he took me to Denny's. While eating a Grand Slam, I realized we were checking out the same cute guy at another table. There were other clues too. Like he hardly ever dated, and he'd never had a serious relationship with a girl. So at Denny's I plain out asked him. He said, "Yeah, I am. But if you tell anyone, I'll kill you."

"That's cool," I said. It is cool. I get it. My super-conservative family will totally freak if they find out. We always got along great, but since then, Mike and I talk about pretty much everything. No subjects are off limits.

After dinner I help clean the kitchen. Then I look for Uncle Mike in the living room. He's not there. I walk down the hallway. His door is open a crack. I push it the rest of the way. He's sitting on his bed reading a textbook. Wearing bright orange earplugs.

I wave to get his attention. He pulls out the plugs and smiles. "Hi, Gassy."

"Hi, Micro." I sit next to him and lean my head on his shoulder.

"Bad day?" he asks.

"Super sucky day."

"Me too. I'm thinking of hiring a female escort to these family dinners."

I look at him. "Still not enough money to move out?"

He shakes his head. "Long way to go." Then he sighs. "I feel lonelier than a pig in a chicken coop."

I laugh. "Lonelier than a what?"

He shrugs. "Don't question. My mind is messed up."

I punch his arm. "It is not. You're brilliant. The best uncle ever."

He wraps his arm around my shoulder and squeezes. "Thanks, Gabs. Tell me about your sucky day."

I think about it. "That pig in the chicken coop thing?"

"Lonely, huh?"

I nod.

"That bites."

"Yeah. It does."

CHAPTER

8

It's Saturday morning, not even eight o'clock. I'm barely awake. The two hours working with Hutch yesterday were so bad, I thought about quitting. But here I am, walking across the warehouse parking lot. I've decided to give it one full day before I tell my parents *no mas trabajo*.

The brick is back in the door. No buzzer. Thank you, God. I reach to pull the door open when I hear, "Good morning," behind me. I'm totally relieved to see it's Evan and not Hutch.

"Hi," I answer.

His shoulders are sagging. Dark circles shadow his eyes. He's gripping a cup of McDonald's coffee like it's a precious elixir. He shoves the door open with his foot. "After you."

I slip inside and he follows me.

Like a robot on autopilot, he walks up to a machine

hanging on the wall. Picks out a yellow card from a rack. Pushes the card into the machine, which goes *ka-chunk*. He slips the card back in its slot, leans against the wall, and closes his eyes. Sips his coffee.

I've seen enough hangovers. I figure that's what he's got. Even though I hate to disturb him, I think I'd better. "Um ... am I supposed to use that machine?"

He opens one eye. Says slowly, "No one told you about the time clock?"

I shake my head.

He shakes his head.

He steps over to it, scans the yellow cards, and pulls one out. Then he ka-chunks it into the time clock. "Gotta do that to get paid," he mutters. He returns to his wall-holding position.

"What about yesterday? I worked two hours!"

He cringes. "Quiet! Work it out with Jake." Then he says, "I didn't mean to snap. The caffeine hasn't hit my bloodstream yet."

The door flies open. In sprints Jo. "Crap, crap, crap!" With a quick glance at the timecards, she picks one out and slams it into the clock. *Ka-chunk.* "Crap."

She slides the card back in its slot. Takes a deep breath. "God, my head hurts." She looks at me. "Hi. It's Gabby, right?"

"Right."

"Good memory," Evan says, his eyes closed. "I forgot." He opens one eye at me. "Sorry." He takes a long drink from his cup.

I shrug.

"Is this your first day?" Jo asks.

"No. Yesterday."

Evan pops both eyes open. He and Jo exchange a glance.

Jo says, "You trained with Hutch?"

"Uh, yeah," I say.

Evan gives me that lopsided grin. "And you're back at work today? Wow. I guess that explains the time clock."

"Hutch is a jerk," Jo says. "Ex-biker, ex-Marine, ex-con."

"Ex-human being," Evan adds. "Oh, and he loves this job." Evan stretches his arms out and groans. "And I love coffee!"

"So, um, did you guys party last night or something?" I ask.

"Friday night? Duh," Evan says.

Jo smiles. "Most nights. Duh."

Evan empties his coffee cup in a long gulp. He wanders toward the office. Throws the cup in a trash can. "Yo, J-man!" he calls.

A second later, Jake walks out of his office. He's carrying a piece of paper. "Morning." He scratches under his Dodger's cap. "Big Eddelsten shipment this afternoon."

Jo whispers in my ear, "Canned goods."

"Otherwise, same old." Jake holds the page in the air. "Who wants this?"

Jo and Evan hesitate. Then Jo snatches it.

"Okay, get to it." Jake turns for his office then twists around. Looks at Jo. "You've been late a few days in a row."

"I know," she says.

"Well … stop it."

"Right, boss." She salutes.

He tugs the brim of his cap.

Jo shows me the page. Looks like a computer printout. Names and numbers. I don't understand any of it.

"Stocking sheet," Jo informs me. "Stuff the store needs from the warehouse."

And that's how my workday begins. Stocking shelves with Jo. The printout starts to make sense once we're using it—aisle number, product name and code, amount needed. Jo never makes me feel like an idiot. Even when I ask what I think are idiotic questions. It's a major improvement from yesterday. I actually feel like I'm learning something.

We're in the warehouse loading a cart with packs of paper towels. Neither of us say much. But it's a comfortable quiet, just working together, getting stuff done. It's nice not having to listen to Randi whining about her boyfriend. Or my parents nagging me about school.

Suddenly Jo says, "Hey, lunchtime."

"Really?" I ask.

"I know, it's totally fun stocking shelves, right? You can keep working if you want."

My cheeks warm. "No, that's okay." But I am surprised how fast the morning went.

We grab sandwiches from the Grocery Mart deli. Jo, Evan, and I park ourselves at a picnic table behind the warehouse. Evan was helping to unload a truck all morning. I guess his hangover is gone. He's all angular lines and hyper energy again.

"So, Gabby," he asks. "Do you talk a lot or something?"

"Ha-ha," I say. I've heard that joke all my life.

"It's short for Gabriella, right?" Jo asks.

I nod.

"Pretty name," she says.

"I guess." I've heard that all my life too. For me, a name is just a name. But I'll play along. "Jo is short for … Josefina?"

"Joelle."

"Oh. That's nice. And Evan is for … Evan."

"Yeah," Evan mutters. "That's as short as it gets. Call me Ev and I kill you." The threat includes a crooked smile.

I can't help smiling back. Our eyes meet. His gaze slides down to my lips before going back to his sandwich. The lingering look leaves a tingling in my belly. How old is Evan? Younger than Uncle Mike, I think. But older than eighteen if he's working full time.

Jo says, "Big plans tonight, Gabby?"

I'm so focused on Evan, her question startles me. "Oh. Not really. I'm grounded." I cringe inside. Did I just say grounded? It sounds so … teen.

Jo laughs. "Really? You seem pretty wholesome. Like you never get in trouble."

"I get into trouble all the time." I'm not smiling when I say it. I don't want them to think I'm some little kid.

"Ooh," Evan murmurs. "All the time." I feel him looking at me again. It makes me squirm. I keep my eyes on my turkey sandwich.

"Do you get into trouble for partying?" Jo asks.

"Maybe," I lie. It's one of the few things I haven't been punished for. Partly because I haven't gotten caught. Mostly because I haven't partied much.

"We're having a little get together at Jo's tonight," Evan says. "If you want to take the chance."

I shrug my shoulders. "Maybe."

Before I clock out that afternoon, Jo writes her address on a piece of paper. I stuff it in my pocket, just to be polite. I have no intention of going.

CHAPTER

9

I hear people complain about buses all the time. They're crowded and stinky. They're never on time. The drivers are rude. It's all true. And I would rather drive a car. But as long as I don't have a car to drive, I'm okay with Rabid Transit. It gives me time to veg.

The bus has just come to another stop. A bunch of people get off and on. I take a deep breath and rest my elbow on the ledge under the window. For the heck of it, I imagine sneaking out of the house tonight. It would be easy. I've done it a bunch of times. Especially when Tony and I first discovered we were more than just friends. We'd camp out behind the metal shed in my backyard and make out. For hours. We haven't done that in a long time.

I press my chin on my hand. The bus starts moving again. Getting to Jo's wouldn't be a problem, either. When she gave me her address, I didn't have to ask for directions.

Her apartment building is less than a mile from my house. An easy walk.

The bus bounces. I lower my hand to my lap. The thing is, I hardly know Jo and Evan. They're older than me. Even so, they treat me like an equal, not a kid. It's kind of how I feel around Uncle Mike. Plus, I like Jo. She's nice. Fun. I think I can trust her. I like Evan too. I'm not so sure I can trust him, but he does seem like fun. I deserve to have fun. I don't deserve to be a prisoner in my house.

My corner is next. I reach up and yank the cord. The bell dings. As I walk the five blocks home, I see a couple of kids shooting baskets in their driveway. The room in my brain that hides things opens for a split second. I catch a glimpse of the basketball tournament. I see me playing. I feel how much I really want to be there. I quickly close the door. In its place I stuff images of Randi telling me we're not friends anymore. Of my teammates in the lunchroom pointing at me, laughing. My parents telling me I'm not as good as my sister.

I need something new.

I figure finding Jo's apartment in this big complex should be easy. Just listen for the loud music. But that pretty much describes every unit of the Ramona Heights apartments. Rap, rock, and salsa pound from behind open and closed doors. I pull the note out of my pocket: 236. I check the number above the closest door: 134. She must be on the second floor. I look up.

A familiar form leans against the upstairs railing. Evan is holding a can of beer and smoking. He gazes into the distance. He looks … good. Can't say I've ever noticed a guy's jaw before. But from this angle I see how perfect his is. Square. Strong.

It's like he feels me staring. He suddenly looks down at me. "Hey, it's Talks-a-lot. Didn't think you were coming. It's kind of late."

"Yeah. Hi." I couldn't leave until after my parents went to bed, around eleven. But I won't tell Evan that. I want him to think I have other places to go. Other people to see.

He flicks his cigarette butt over the railing. It lands on the cement not far from my feet. "Come on up," he says.

I find the stairs and make my way down the second-floor hallway. Evan has disappeared. The door to 236 is closed. The base track of an R&B song thumps from inside. I feel timid all of a sudden. Then I tell myself, "You're here to have fun. So … have fun."

Taking a deep breath, I reach for the knob. Wait, should I knock? The door opens.

"There you are," Jo says, smiling. She grabs my hand and pulls me inside. "This is Gabby," she announces. There are a whole lot of people scattered around. They're draped on the couch. Lounging on the floor. Milling in the kitchen.

Someone says, "Hey."

Someone else waves.

Then they go back to whatever they were doing. Which seems to be drinking and smoking pot and making out. A bong is getting passed around.

"Booze in the kitchen," Jo says. "Help yourself."

"Hey, are you twenty-one?" a guy asks me with a snicker. He barely looks older than I am.

"Shut up, Andy," Jo says. She goes to the couch and sits across two laps—a guy's and a girl's. Okay.

I head to the kitchen, stepping over legs and a torso. Evan is in front of the refrigerator. He opens it and hands me a beer. "Want a shot with that?" He points to the bottles of hard stuff on the counter.

"No. That's okay." I grab the beer and take a long swig. Then a couple more.

"In a hurry?" he asks.

"Um …" I let out an awkward laugh. "Maybe."

He squints. "So how old are you?"

"Eighteen." I don't miss a beat. I'm getting good at lying. As long as he brought it up, I ask, "How old are you?"

"Twenty-two. Think that's too big an age difference?"

I shrug. "For what?"

Grinning, he reaches out and tucks a strand of hair behind my ear. "You are incredibly cute." He's staring at my face like I'm an ice cream cone and he wants to lick me.

I don't know what to say. Or do. This is so strange. I just met him a couple days ago. It took Tony years to make his first move. Evan wraps his hand around the back of my neck. My skin tingles where he touches me. My toes curl. He pulls me to his lips and I let him. It's just a brush of a kiss. The barest of touches. Then he lets go.

I don't realize my eyes are closed until I open them. He's smiling down at me. "Sorry," he says. "Didn't mean to interrupt your beer drinking."

"That's … okay." I take another gulp. I finally start to feel the alcohol. The room floats a little. It's a nice feeling. I smile at Evan. I smile at the girl who tugs Evan's wrist and leads him away. I smile when I take a hit off the bong and drink a shot of tequila. I smile when Lance, a friend of Jo's, drives me home. I even smile when I see Tony waiting for me on my front steps.

CHAPTER

10

Lance is just pulling away from the curb when I see Tony. At least, I think it's Tony. My vision is a little blurry.

I stand there a second, waiting for the walkway to stop moving like water. It doesn't. I'm going to have to cross a cement ocean to get to my house. I wonder if there are fish swimming in the sidewalk. I take a wobbly step and laugh.

Hey, it is Tony. He's walking toward me. Why is he here? And doesn't he know he might drown? "Careful," I say.

"What?" he whispers.

Why is he whispering?

He grabs my elbow.

I pull it back. "What are you doing?"

"Helping you to the house." He hisses the words through his teeth. He sounds like a snake. He doesn't look like a snake. But he's frowning. His eyes are narrowed.

"You're pissed off," I say.

He takes a deep breath. "I can help you to the house. Or I can leave you here. Which do you want?"

Why is he making me choose? I don't like choosing. "I don't know," I tell him.

He slowly takes my elbow again. He's gentler now. I don't pull back. He tugs a little. I go with him. Like a little old lady. Like a grandma. I see us in the future, two old people walking home.

"Do you love me?" I ask. We're halfway to the steps.

"Yes," he says.

"Why?"

He doesn't answer.

"Hey!" I blurt out. Throw my arm around him. "Want to make out behind the shed?"

"That's not a good idea." He whispers so low I barely hear him. "If you aren't quiet, Raul and Yolanda will wake up."

Raul and Yolanda. My parents. If they wake up … If they wake up, they'll kill me. Do I want them to kill me? I don't know. I don't think so. I really hate choosing.

We've reached the first step. I stop. It's a long way up to the porch. Then I remember. This isn't how I left earlier. I left through my window. "I have to climb through my window," I say.

Tony shakes his head.

I unwrap my arm from him. "My window, Tony."

"You're too drunk. You might hurt yourself."

"I won't."

"I'll help you up the steps. But I won't help you through your window."

"Okay. Bye."

He throws his hands up like he's done with me. Walks away.

I stagger to the side of the house. My stomach heaves and I throw up in the bushes.

Early morning sunlight wakes me. I'm lying on my side in the dirt next to the house. I get to my feet. Pushing my window open as quietly as I can, I climb inside.

I lay my head on my pillow. Images from the party swirl behind my eyes. Drinking. Laughing. Kissing Evan. I kissed somebody else too. Kirk … Kevin? Whoever he was, I think he felt me up. Tony was here last night. He helped me get to the house. I should have kissed him good night.

I fall asleep kissing Tony.

There's a knock on my door. I quickly pull my blanket up to my chin to make sure my clothes are covered. Mom walks in. "Half an hour to Mass."

I groan. The vibration of my voice hurts my head. "I'm not going. I'm sick."

"You've been sleeping over twelve hours."

"No, I haven't."

She's silent.

"I was sick during the night. I think it was something I ate."

"We all ate the same dinner. No one else is sick." She stands over my bed and stares at me. My hair is probably matted. I must look pale, because I feel pale.

"Okay," she says with a sigh. "Just this once."

I try to doze as the Herrera household gets ready. Do they have to be so loud? The front door closes. It's so quiet I can't sleep. Half an hour later I'm in the shower. Then I'm in the yard, hosing away my puke.

By the time the front door opens again, I'm sitting at the kitchen table. Trying to work my way through a bowl of cereal. It's not easy.

"How are you feeling?" I look up. It's Tony. He's come in with the rest of my family.

"Not so good," I answer.

"Can we talk a minute?" His lips are smiling, but his eyes aren't.

I leave my bowl on the table and lead him out the back door. We sit on the kiddie swings. I hold the chains. Start to twist my swing like I always do. But the movement makes me feel sick. I face forward, slumping my shoulders against the chains.

Tony says, "I want to ask where you were last night. Who you were with. But I know it's none of my business."

"I was with the guys from work. Joelle and Evan. They invited me to a party."

He shuffles his feet in the dirt. "Okay."

"I didn't invite you because they didn't say I could. They only invited me." This is a lie. And lame. Unless it's a slumber party, no one cares if you bring a boyfriend to a party. I know it. Tony knows it.

He stares into the yard. "I'm wondering if we should break up."

I lean my head against the chains. It's going to be another weirdly hot day. It's only eleven and heat waves are already shimmering above the lawn.

"Did you hear me?" he asks.

I nod.

"So?"

"So … okay," I say softly.

He pauses. "Okay we should break up?"

I slowly nod again.

Tony sits there a few seconds. Then in a flash of movement he's up and gone.

His swing clangs against the metal support post. I watch as it wavers back and forth, back and forth until it finally stops.

I want to sit out here forever. I want to get really hot and sweat out what's left of the alcohol, the drugs, Kurt or Kevin and his traveling hands. But it's just too painful. I walk into the house.

CHAPTER

11

Of all the crappy changes in my life, the one crappy constant is homework. It never goes away.

I'm sitting at my desk Sunday night. I've taken a billion pain relievers. I think my hangover headache is finally giving in. I'm finishing up my literature paper that was due last week. At first I feel good it's getting done. I print it out and read it over. I'm not sure I covered all the points I was supposed to. It might be worth a B. But since it's late, Mrs. Mosley won't give me full credit. So it's probably a C paper. Crap. So much for raising my grade. I shove the report into my notebook.

I pull out my geometry book and worksheet. Well, what do you know? The worksheet is full of triangles. Friggin' stupid triangles. I don't give a crap how many degrees each corner has. Pythagoras is a stupid name, anyway. Pissy Gord Ass.

Hah! I reach for my phone to text Randi.

Crap.

I rest my elbows on the desk. Then press my head in my hands. I grab handfuls of hair and tug. Tug. Tug. It's like the hair-tugging releases the latch on my brain room. There's Tony. He's reaching out to me. With his puppy-dog eyes. Get back, Tony. Breaking up was the right thing to do. We're not good together. You're as exciting as an avocado pit. I'm serious. Get back. I see him slowly turn around and walk through the door. I slam it shut.

I take a deep breath. Close my book. Leave my room. In the hallway I yell, "Mom, can I use your car? I want to go to Abuelita's."

"Is your homework done?"

"Yes."

Five-second pause. "Take your sisters."

"What? No!"

Silence.

"All right!" I say. "Crap."

"Gabriella!"

Rosie and Marta fight all the way to Grandma's. They're so noisy I want to scream. I was never that loud when I was ten and twelve. They park themselves in front of the TV when we get there. Fine. Good riddance.

Grandma is in grandkid heaven and trots into the kitchen to make popcorn.

I knock on Uncle Mike's door. He opens it. His eyes widen when he sees me.

"Hey," he says. "Are you okay?"

I shake my head, already crying.

He wraps me in his arms. I sob.

I wake up on Uncle Mike's bed. I must have talked and cried myself to sleep. There's a blanket covering me. He's sitting at his desk. A couple of textbooks are open on either side of his laptop.

"Hi," I mumble. "Was I out long?"

He swivels his chair around. "Hi. Close to an hour."

"What are you working on?"

He glances at his desk. "Pharmacology."

I sit up, wrapping the blanket around me. "That sounds hard."

He shrugs. "It is. But I can't graduate without it."

Uncle Mike is in a community-college nursing program. It took him three years to finish all the prereqs. Then another couple years on the program's waiting list. All that time he's been working as a practical nurse in an old folks' home. He's got the Herrera family ambition. But he's not preachy about it.

He grabs a pencil off his desk and pokes into it with

his thumbnail. "Gabs. I know the last thing you want is a lecture. But you need to be careful with the alcohol and stuff."

Okay. Maybe he's a little preachy. "I know."

He stares at me.

"I said I know."

"Even if you're not on the basketball team anymore, can you go to some of the games? Maybe do stuff with Randi again?"

I pull the blanket snug around my chest. "We're not friends anymore."

"Are you sure? Maybe if you were, you know, nicer—"

I glare at him.

He smiles. "You don't always think before you talk, Gabs. I'm telling you this because I love you."

If this was anyone but Uncle Mike, I'd be walking out. I'm hot all of a sudden and throw the blanket off.

"Do you hate me now?" he asks.

"No."

We're both quiet for a minute. Once I've cooled down, I look over at him. He's slouched in his chair, studying the pencil again and frowning.

"What's wrong?" I ask.

He shrugs.

I sigh. "I told you my crap. Your turn."

He seems to think about it. "I'm not doing so good

with my classes this semester. I have to keep a B average or they'll kick me out. And I'm getting mostly Cs."

"What? But you always work so hard."

"Yeah, well … sometimes hard work isn't enough."

"But you'll turn your grades around, right?"

"Sure." I can tell he doesn't believe it.

"Uncle Mike, you have to! So you can move out of here."

He nods and flips the pencil onto his desk. "That's not all." He sighs. "I got into a thing with Alex. The local newspaper interviewed him about the campus LGBT club. Alex mentioned me by name. I'm not officially in the club, but I go to their events. Alex told me the story was published this morning."

Alex is his boyfriend. I instantly get why Uncle Mike is worried. "I don't think anyone in our family reads that paper."

"I don't think so, either. But what if one of their friends or someone they work with does?"

"Oh. Right. What are you going to do?"

"I may have to tell everyone. Officially come out."

I can't imagine what will happen. But if the family finds out from a newspaper article, it could be worse. "That may be the best."

"Think so?"

I nod.

"You're probably right. Guess it's time to step up and be brave."

"You might feel better about yourself." But when I think about it, I'm not sure that's true. I have no idea what he's going through. Poor Mike. No wonder he's struggling with his classes. I walk over and press my hand on his shoulder. "It'll be okay."

"Yeah." He pats my hand.

The door flies open and Marta barges in. "Mom called. She wants to know why we're not home yet."

"Hey, douchebag. Ever heard of knocking?"

Uncle Mike gives me a look.

I smile at him. "Okay. Be nice. I get it." I take a deep breath. "Call me on the home phone. You know, if you need to talk or something."

"Same to you," he says.

I pet Marta's head. "Come along, darling sister."

She looks up like I'm crazy and runs off.

I shrug at Uncle Mike as I leave. But he's not looking. He's grabbed the pencil from his desk. Rolling it between his fingers. He's bent at the waist, arms on his knees. It's like a huge weight is pushing him down, down, down. Crushing his shoulders. The sight makes me so sad.

CHAPTER

12

I'm still thinking about Uncle Mike when I head for school the next morning. Then, as I get closer to campus, I start thinking about me. About being nice and reconnecting to Randi. Part of me believes being nice is bull. If I'm not nice to someone, they don't deserve it. But I know I've hurt people's feelings. And it's because of what Uncle Mike said. Stuff comes out of my mouth before my brain figures out the best thing to say.

So should I try to make it right with Randi again? I've just gotten to the main hallway. I see her in front of her locker. I hesitate. Start to make my way through the crowd. But when I look up again, she's already leaving. I don't bother trying to catch up.

When lunch rolls around, I stand at the checkout counter for a second. I glance at our table. The same guys are sitting there. I grab my burrito and juice off my tray. Go outside.

Sit by myself under a tree. I know Randi is at the team table. I know they're talking about Saturday's tournament. The awesome three-pointers. The amazing blocks and rebounds. The bitches on the other teams.

I bite into my burrito and figure something out—why only team members sit at that table. For one, outsiders don't have a clue what they're talking about. It's basketball talk, all the time. And two, the Crusaders like it that way. They don't like outsiders. I connect the dots. The picture it makes is me, sitting alone under a tree.

What the picture doesn't show is the burrito knocking around inside my stomach. Like a sneaker in a washing machine. I wrap up what's left and throw it away.

I find my timecard: Herrera, Gabriella.

Ka-chunk.

My official third day of work has begun. Is it lame when your job is the only thing you look forward to? I'm not even going to answer that.

Beep-beep-beep.

Big Bird backs out of aisle three. Jo is driving. She's carrying a pallet of boxes, *Campbell's* printed on the sides. Soup, row *D*. Hmm, I guess this isn't rocket science.

Jo looks over and sees me. Smiles and waves. I wave back. I see Evan pushing a handcart through the double doors into the store. I admire his lanky build and muscly shoulders. He's got a nice butt too. Don't know as I noticed that before.

I remember our kiss. The barely there lip touch that curled my toes. I don't think it meant anything. A few seconds later he hooked up with another girl. Someone older than me. And prettier.

But the thing about barely there kisses? They leave you wanting more. A completely there kiss. I shove that kiss back where it belongs. In the room in my brain that hides things. I shut the door. Only it doesn't close completely. Like there's a foot stuck in the jamb. I shove the door a few times. Give up.

I take a deep breath. There's a light on in the office. Jake is sitting at his desk, staring at his computer.

"Hi," I say.

He looks up. "Hey. How's it going? I notice you didn't clock in or out Friday."

"I was here—"

"Yeah, Hutch told me. Just make sure you always use the clock. The paperwork is a hassle if you don't."

"Okay." I don't add that a-hole Hutch didn't tell me about the clock.

Jake is staring at his computer screen again.

"So, um, what do you want me to do?"

"Ask Jo or Evan. Or Hutch, when he's on the floor.

Late afternoons and Saturdays are the busiest times for the store. You're here to back them up."

"Okay." I head off to find Jo or Evan.

I run into Evan first. He's returning to the store with the empty pushcart.

He gives me a beaming smile. "Hey, Talks-a-lot. I wasn't sure you'd be back. Thought maybe we scared you Saturday night."

I shrug. "I can handle a party."

"That's what I told Jo. She was worried. Especially letting you ride home with Lance. He was pretty loaded."

He was? I don't remember.

"Well, since you survived, I need to tell you Kevin is interested."

Kevin? Oh right. Mr. Happy Hands. I shake my head. "No. I don't think so."

Evan nods, like it's the right answer. "Good. He's a jerk. And a lousy kisser. That's what I hear, anyway." The flirty smile Evan gives me could register on that earthquake scale.

Uh. Wow. I can't take my eyes off his mouth.

Glancing around the warehouse, he reaches into his pocket. Pulls out a small, flat container. Unscrews the lid and takes a sip. "Want a swig? Helps the time pass."

He's drinking at work? I hesitate a second. Then take

the bottle and sip. It burns my throat. I cough and laugh as I hand it back to him. "That's strong."

"Vodka. No odor." Then he says, "Can you help stock soup in the store? Aisle twelve?"

"Sure."

I don't see much of Evan or Jo for the rest of my shift. It's pretty much the same routine Tuesday. I walk to school. Do school. Take the bus to work. Do work. Get a nice buzz off Evan's vodka. Ride home with Mom. Do home stuff. Go to bed. Sleep. Worry about Uncle Mike. But since he hasn't called, I figure he's okay.

Wednesday's the same thing up to the doing-home-stuff part. I'm sitting in my room. After I worry about Uncle Mike, I try not to think about basketball. Tonight the Crusaders are playing the Solano Academy Chiefs. I memorized the game schedule at the beginning of the season. I can't suddenly unmemorize it. I always love playing the Chiefs. Our schools are big rivals, especially in basketball. We get really hyped up. I can picture Coach Matthews's red face as she gives us a last-minute pep talk. Me, bouncing on my toes, my nerves all jittery. Randi laughing, telling me to calm down.

All that adrenalin. The yelling. Screaming. It's crazy. Acting out without getting into trouble. When you've got six arms all slapping at you. Not wanting you to make that basket. And that feeling when the ball obeys you anyway. Swooshes through the net. It's … amazing. Such a rush.

I'm good at basketball. I am good at it. Like I've never been good at anything. I miss it so much. And I can't believe I'm not playing tonight.

When I sneak out of the house, I'm not sure what's going through my head. I mean, I know I can't play. I think I just want to be there.

CHAPTER

13

I stand in the locker room, just outside the gym. Listen to players yelling. Shouts from the crowd. The echoey *boing-boing-boing* of the ball dribbling down the wooden floor.

Coach Matthews cries, "Shoot, Johnson!"

A groan from the fans. Shawnie Johnson must have missed her shot. Or lost the ball. It's sounds like there's a pretty big crowd tonight. That's cool. Crowds always help us play better.

I want to be inside. But I'll feel lame if anyone sees me. Like I don't have a life. Like I wish I was playing. I do wish I was playing. I just don't want them to think I do. Like I'm desperate.

Slipping through the door, I hide next to the bleachers. I'm on the Crusader's side of the court. No one from our bench can see me. The guys on the court can, but they've got other stuff to watch. Randi's under the basket. She grabs a rebound. Lays it up, but the ball hits the rim. A Chief grabs the ball, takes it down the court. They score. Crap.

I glance at the scoreboard. The Crusaders are down 35 to 42. They're in the second half. Not so good.

"C'mon, guys," I say under my breath.

Alicia passes to Tiana. She passes to Celeste. Celeste tosses from the three-point line. It hangs in the air, hits the rim, and goes through.

"Yes!" I punch my fist.

Every play, every block, every run down the court, my muscles twitch. I'm out there with my team, dribbling, making those shots. The Crusaders fight back. Tie the score. Randi is under the basket again. She misses a layup. Grabs the ball.

"C'mon, Randi!" I scream.

Her rebound goes in this time. Nice. She looks over. Sees me. I can't read her expression. Surprise, maybe? She panting, sweating. Runs back down the court.

It's a tight game. A great game. Two minutes left. I should slip out. Randi saw me, but no one else has. It would be like I was never here. But I can't leave. A good player doesn't desert her team.

The score shifts back and forth. Ten seconds. Five seconds. The crowd gets on their feet. Coach Matthews is screaming. Bench players are standing, screaming. Tiana gets the ball. She shoots. The buzzer blares. The ball rises, arcs, sinks.

Score!

The Crusaders win by a point. I'm crying. I can't help it. I sprint through the locker room. I run outside, still crying. At first it's a happy cry. I'm happy we won. I'm surprised how happy I am. But as I run home, the cry turns into something else. More like a wail. Like someone is reaching into my chest and ripping out my heart.

Instead of climbing quietly through my bedroom window, I barge through the front door. The TV is on. Marta and Rosie look up from the couch. Their eyes are wide. I must look crazy. I'm panting, sweating, still crying.

My parents are standing in the kitchen, talking. Arms crossed. Serious expressions. They look at me when I walk in. Mom's jaw drops a little.

I don't slow down. I walk right up to Dad. Pull my hand back. Slap him. It's a hard slap. My fingers sting. I reach back to hit him again but he grabs my wrist. Holds tight.

I'm glaring at him. He glares back, his face red. He's hurting my wrist, but I don't want to show it. I roll my hand into a fist.

"Gabriella," Mom gasps.

I could just as easily have hit her. But she wasn't the one who said, *y no mas baloncesto* a week ago. This was his idea.

"*Cabrón!*" I hiss into Dad's face. Bastard.

He slaps my cheek with his free hand. My head reels.

The blow forces my eyes away for a second. Then I'm snapping my head back, glaring at him.

He's breathing hard. Studying my face like he's trying to figure out what just walked into his kitchen and attacked him.

"Basketball was everything to me," I explain. "And you took it away."

He closes his eyes. Shakes his head in disgust, like, *Friggin' basketball again*? He lets go of my wrist. Yells, "When will you learn to take responsibility, Gabriella! You sneak out of the house. Refuse to study. Break up with Antonio." He shakes his head again. He is so, so disappointed in me.

"Don't even talk about Tony. Who I date is my business."

He points. "Go to your room!"

He doesn't get it. He just. Does not. Get it. I'm not a real person to him. I'm a broken person. A broken Herrera. Like the nurses dropped me on my head when I was born. I take a deep breath, my anger spent. I turn and walk away.

Halfway through the living room, Dad calls, "You're not allowed to talk to your uncle."

I twist around. "What?"

"You are not to call or see Uncle Mike."

"Why? Is this my punishment for hitting you?"

Dad doesn't answer. His mouth is twisted, grim. There's

something else going on. Dad's eyes are steady, but Mom's are downcast. Sad. And it hits me. They were doing some serious talking when I walked in. Did Uncle Mike come out to Grandma? And now Dad is, what … shunning him?

I think so. I think Dad means no one in our family is allowed to talk to Uncle Mike. Not just me.

Dad doesn't know I know. I could get into with him. Ask him a bunch of questions. Make him scramble for answers. Since no answer he comes up with will ever make sense. But I'm done with my father. Just … done. I walk to my room and close the door. I need to talk to Uncle Mike.

CHAPTER

14

Rosie is twelve. She's also a parental suck-up. After watching me and Celia, she's figured out how to work the system. Act like an angel, then do what you want behind their backs. Six months before she turned twelve, she started doing extra chores around the house. Finished all her homework. Got As and Bs. Never talked back. Two months before her birthday she started asking for a cell phone. No way that was going to happen. Mom and Dad had this rule about no cell phones until *quinceañera*.

The little suck-up got her way. They gave her a phone for being such a good girl. But Rosie is not the mini Celia they think she is. I've smelled dope on her clothes. I've seen her hanging out with boys at the mall, hands all over each other. It pisses me off that she gets away with crap. But in a way I don't care. I've got my life. She's got hers. We all have our methods for getting by.

Tonight, I'm glad Rosie is a suck-up. I need to borrow her phone.

She and Marta are still watching TV in the living room. I slip into their bedroom. Search Rosie's backpack. Not there. Look around. It's on her desk. I carry it back to my bedroom. She doesn't have Uncle Mike's cell number coded in like I do. It takes me a few seconds to remember it. He answers after one ring.

"Rosie?" he asks.

"No, Uncle Mike. It's Gabby. Did you tell Grandma?"

He sighs. "Yeah." He doesn't say anything else.

"So, what happened?"

More silence. Then, "It's not good. She's kicking me out of the house."

"You're kidding me! Where will you go?"

"I don't know."

"Can you move in with Alex?"

"No. I confronted him about naming me in the article. He said he did it on purpose. To force me to come out. I broke up with him."

"Oh crap." Then I quietly say, "Dad knows. He says I can't talk to you."

"Yeah. Looks like the whole family has pretty much disowned me. I'm a walking sin."

I feel sick to my stomach. This is partly my fault. "I'm sorry. I shouldn't have told you to do it."

"Hey, you didn't know this would happen. It was my decision anyway."

I grip the phone. Maybe I didn't know it would happen. But I knew it could. "So, where will you go?"

"I'm thinking the army."

"Seriously? But you're almost done with your nursing program."

"It'll be hard to finish college figuring out a place to live."

We're both quiet a few seconds. Then he says, "Look, you'd better hang up. You don't want to get in trouble with your dad."

"I don't care."

"You should care, Gabby. You don't want to end up on the street."

"I'm going to come and see you," I say.

"Don't risk it. I'm like kryptonite."

"Not to me."

After a moment of silence, he says, "Thanks, Gabs. I love you. Bye." He ends the call.

I'm standing in the middle of my room, holding Rosie's phone, feeling like the floor is falling away. Then I notice the absence of sound. No TV. Water starts running in the bathroom. I need to return Rosie's phone. I sneak back to my sisters' bedroom. Rosie is sitting on her bed, alone.

I hand her the phone and whisper, "You tell Dad I used this and you're dead."

I can see her brain working. She just saw me slap Dad. She knows I'm serious. She nods quickly and takes the phone. She looks up. "So Uncle Mike is gay? I heard Dad and Mom talking."

"Yeah, he is. Do you even know what that means?"

"Of course. I'm not a dummy." Then she says, "I'm sorry about what's happening. I don't believe all that stuff they say in church. I don't think gay people are bad. You can use my phone if you want to call him again."

I hesitate. "Thanks."

"I'm sorry about basketball too. I know you really liked it."

I can tell Rosie means what she says. I also know she's counting on me not to rat her out the next time I see her with a boy or smoking dope. She doesn't have to worry. I won't. I nod and go back to my room.

I don't sleep very well that night. Mom and Dad open my door at all hours to make sure I haven't snuck out. My dreams are a mess. At one point I'm at the gym watching Uncle Mike make a basket. Then I borrow Dad's phone to tell Randi. Suddenly, Tony is using Dad's cell to text me. He drops it next to the swings. Evan drives over it with the forklift. I hear the phone crunch and snap apart. The crunching sound wakes me. I sit up, look around. But it was just a dream.

All day, I try to figure out a way to get to Uncle Mike's. I could take the bus after school. But I'm feeling weirdly attached to my job and don't want to lose it. I think of asking Mom to drive us to Abuelita's before we go home. But there's no way she'll go for that, not with Dad so pissy about me seeing his brother.

The best I can do is borrow Rosie's phone again and call Uncle Mike. Which I do after dinner. He doesn't pick up. I call for the next few hours, each time leaving the same message: "Hey. It's Gabby. Call me."

I even text him, although he's old school and doesn't text much. I hide the phone under my pillow, on vibrate so it doesn't wake anyone. When he doesn't call, I tell myself he's busy finding a new place to live. Or he's at the army recruiter's office. But I'm worried that he hasn't called.

The next day, Friday, I go through the same routine. I borrow Rosie's phone and call Uncle Mike after dinner. This time, he picks up right away.

"Gabby?" he asks.

"Yes!" I let out a breath. "Are you okay?"

"Um, yeah. I feel pretty good, actually." His voice is light. I don't think he's faking it. He sounds happier than I've heard him in a long time. A really long time.

"Wow. That's great."

"Yeah. Things are kind of falling into place." Then he says, "Hey, I'm sorting through some stuff in my bedroom.

I've got a cardboard box with your name on it. Just a few things I can't take with me. I want you to have them."

"Um … okay—"

"Listen, I have to run, Gabby. Lots to do. Take care of yourself, okay? I love you. I love you a lot."

"I love you too, but—"

He's already hung up.

15

Friday night I sleep like crap again. I'm feeling a little better about Uncle Mike. I mean, I'm glad he has someplace to go. Is the army taking him already? He seems happy about it. But I still find myself tossing and turning, thinking about him. Why didn't he give me his new address? I'd like to go see him.

Mom and Dad keep checking my room during the night again. I think they're on a pee schedule. Every time one of them goes to the bathroom, they open my door. I hate feeling like a prisoner.

Saturday snowballs with lateness. I wake up late. Miss the bus. Have to wait twenty minutes for the next one. I'm not even sure why I'm running across the parking lot. It won't make the time clock move back to eight.

Thinking I'm the last person here, I kick the brick out

of the doorway. Slide my timecard into the clock—*ka-chunk*—just as the door slams shut.

"Uh-oh," says a deep voice. "Slippery slope."

I look over. Evan is leaning against the wall, eyes closed. Holding a McDonald's coffee.

I slip my card back in its slot. "What?"

"One late morning leads to two. Pretty soon, you're late more often than you're on time. Before you know it, you're a late-a-holic."

I roll my eyes.

"It's true. Ask Jo."

I look around. "Where is she?"

"Late."

He stretches his arms out and crumples his coffee cup. I don't know how he makes something that ordinary look so graceful. He's like the lions I've seen on videos, stretching before they chase dinner. Or don't chase dinner. If I remember right, female lions do all the work.

There's a pounding and a muffled, "Hey, open the damn door!"

I open the door. Jo bounds in. Fumbles with her card. Slams it in the clock. "Sh—"

"See? Late addict." Evan raises an eyebrow at me.

Jo frowns. "Yeah, three hours of sleep will do that."

"Good party?" I ask. They invited me. If it wasn't for

my prison-guard parents and worrying about Uncle Mike, I would have gone.

"Of course," Jo says.

"You should have come." Evan gives me a leering, lop-sided grin. "I missed you."

"Right."

"I did. Tell her, Jo. Wasn't I crying all night?"

"Yep," says Jo. "His tears watered everyone's beers. It was horrible."

He steps over and stands inches from me. "You're coming tonight, aren't you?"

I can feel the heat from his skin. Smell the coffee and tobacco on his breath. The crazy thing is, I want him to step closer. Smash our bodies together. Press our lips together.

"Please tell me you're coming tonight," he says.

"Hey. Guys," Jo hisses.

Evan steps back. So do I. Jake is marching toward us from his office.

"It's eight fifteen!" Jake yells. "Socialize on your own time." He shoves a printout into Jo's hand. Glares at Evan. Then he looks at me. I can tell he's disappointed. It bothers me a little.

Jo and I walk silently into the store. The morning is taken up with stocking nonalcoholic beverages. Big bottles and six-packs. Then bags of chips and boxes of crackers.

"Must be a big game on TV today," Jo says. "We're not usually this short."

Unlike last Saturday, the morning drags. After working here a week and a half, I've pretty much gotten the hang of things. It was never all that exciting to begin with, but any sparkly newness had worn off.

"I think I get why you're late all the time," I tell Jo as I push more Ritz boxes onto a shelf. "I can't imagine doing this same job forever."

"It's not that bad. And there are perks." She walks down the aisle, looking for spots that need stuff.

"Perks? You mean like health insurance and vacation days?"

"Yeah, but … not exactly."

She looks up and down the aisle, like she doesn't want anyone to hear. Then she steps up next to me and says softly, "You're cool. I can trust you, right? Or poke your eye out with a stick."

I nod.

"Booze," she whispers.

"Booze?"

She gives me a sly smile. Her earrings glisten in the store's bright lights.

I wait for an explanation, but it doesn't come. She goes

back to work. I think about it. What, are they stealing alcohol or something?

Evan and Jo are pretty quiet at lunch. Evan takes out his flask and takes a long swig. "Hair of the dog," he says after he swallows. He holds the bottle out for me. It's not even noon, but I shrug and take it. I drink enough so I'll get a good buzz. It takes the edge off work. I guess it takes the edge off everything.

I glance at Jo. "So you're lifting alcohol from the warehouse?"

Evan coughs as he takes a bite of his sandwich. He glares at Jo.

She shrugs. "It's just Gabby. She won't tell."

"But her mom works here," Evan says.

"That hasn't stopped you from making passes at her."

He snorts. "Whatever." Then he says, "Yeah. We're pinching liquor."

"Okay," I say. "That's cool. I really won't tell anyone."

Late that afternoon I'm cutting boxes. The vodka I've been drinking all afternoon is getting to me. My cuts go kind of wobbly. I have to keep reminding myself to get my fingers out of the way of the blade.

"Gabby?"

I look up. Jake is holding his lunch bag. He's frowning. I sit back on my heels.

He pushes his cap up. "Look. I don't know you all

that well. But you seem like a good kid." He pauses. "Just watch yourself around Evan, okay? He's … older. I think he's been around. If you know what I mean."

I can't believe my boss is lecturing me about Evan. "Um … okay."

He pulls him cap brim down. "So … that's it. See you next week."

"Yeah. See you."

He leaves.

I go back to cutting boxes. Five minutes later, Jo is heading out too. I look at the clock. It's not five yet. She shoves the brick in the doorway. From the loading dock, I hear the electronic door whir as it opens. It stops partway. Curious, I walk to the end of the paper goods aisle. Jo is pulling her old red Miata up next to the loading dock. The trunk pops open. Evan quickly carries out a couple of boxes and drops them into her car. He closes the trunk. As the electronic door closes, I see Jo parking her Miata back in its regular spot.

It can't be that simple … can it? I watch around a shelf as Evan walks to Jake's office. Unlocks the door and sits at the computer. Maybe he's changing the inventory list. So it's not all that simple.

When he's finished, he walks toward me. Holding a bottle. "You didn't just see that."

I smile. "See what?"

He hands the bottle to me. "It's polite to bring something to parties. You are coming to Jo's tonight, right?"

I take the bottle. It's vodka. I think it's the expensive kind. The label looks expensive, anyway. "I ... I can't. There's no way—"

He grabs me by the waist and pulls me against him. He presses his lips against mine, hard this time. A real kiss. A hungry kiss. I kiss him back, just as hard. I know Evan is older than me. I know he's been around. And now I know something bad about Evan that Jake isn't even aware of. I don't even care.

16

After Mom and Dad go to bed, I shove some clothes under the covers. It may not fool them when they do their prison check. But what are they going to do, ground me? Take my phone? I think about bringing the bottle Evan gave me. But leave it behind. I don't like the idea of getting stopped by the cops carrying it.

I walk into Jo's apartment without knocking. It's the same as before: loud music, people sprawled everywhere, a bong getting passed around. A girl near the door says, "Hey." I recognize her from the other party. She's Maria or Marlena or something. I look around for Jo and Evan. Don't see them.

"Where's Jo?" I ask.

"In the back." She holds one side of her nose and inhales. Gives me a knowing smile.

Okay. I make my way to the kitchen. I'm about to open the fridge for a beer, but change my mind. Grab the vodka off the counter. Fill a plastic cup to the brim. I look down the hallway toward the back of the apartment. A couple is making out against the wall, really into it. I take a long drink from my glass. Scoot by, trying not to disturb them. A bedroom door is open.

The sight is a lot to take in. That guy, Kevin, Mr. Happy Hands, is standing in front of a dresser. He's leaning over, snorting a line of white powder through a short straw. Another guy stands next to him, like he's waiting his turn. Then there's Jo and Evan. They're on the bed. Kissing. Groping. I tell myself to look away. This isn't any of my business. Except … it is. I thought Evan was into me. I thought Jo knew Evan was into me. Are they a couple? What's going on?

Kevin turns away from the dresser and sees me. Grins. "Hey, I was hoping you'd show."

Jo looks up. Smiles. "Gabby!"

Then Evan sees me. "Hi, Talks-a-lot."

Neither of them looks ashamed. Like they're doing something they shouldn't.

Evan pats the bed between him and Jo. He gives me a leering smile. "Come here."

He wants me to join them? Is he friggin' kidding me?

By now Kevin has wrapped his arm around my waist. "Want some blow?" He gestures with his chin to the dresser.

I shake my head. Finish off my vodka in a single gulp. Duck underneath Kevin's arm. Retrace my way down the hallway. Past the hot-and-heavy couple. Set the empty cup on the kitchen counter. Jog home.

I crawl through my window. Quickly get under the covers. I lost my virginity two years ago. I'm not a prude. But that was just … weird. At least I think it was weird. I consider asking Uncle Mike. Maybe he has a clue. My head swims. From the vodka and from everything else.

I wake up. The home phone is ringing. Why doesn't someone answer it? I close my eyes.

Ring.

Ring.

I prop myself onto an elbow. Yell, "Will someone please get the phone?"

My head pounds. I didn't think I had all that much to drink. I guess I did. Like … all day. I flop back onto my bed. The ringing finally stops. Thank you.

"Hello?" Mom's voice filters in from her bedroom. She switches to Spanish. Must be a relative.

The sun is blaring through my curtains. It's late. Close to Mass. There's no way I can skip out on church this morning. Not two Sundays in a row. I throw the covers off and slowly get up. My stomach churns. I feel like crap.

Throwing on my robe, I head for the bathroom. Mom is ahead of me, trotting into the kitchen. She never trots.

"Raul!" she cries. "Raul!" She's hysterical.

My heart speeds up.

I clutch my bathrobe around my chest. Follow her. She's gone out the sliding door into the backyard. Dad is watering the shrubs. Mom takes hold of his arm. She's crying, her cheeks glistening wet. She says something. Dad drops the hose. He presses his hand over his mouth and squeezes his eyes shut.

A few minutes later I find out Uncle Mike is dead. He hanged himself in Abuelita's garage.

The rest of the week is like out of a zombie movie. I walk around doing stuff, but my brain is numb. Several times a day I think about calling Uncle Mike. Because I'm sad. Because he'll know the right thing to say. Then I remember he's dead. I'll never see him again. I'll never talk to him again. Ever.

The day of the funeral, distant relatives talk in hushed, gossipy voices. They don't understand why he committed suicide. I hear my dad tell one of his cousins that Mike was failing his nursing program. He couldn't handle the stress. But no one talks about the real reason Uncle Mike was stressed. Because his family rejected him for being gay. That he couldn't just be who he was.

Dad is devastated. His eyes have been red and teary since he found out. I know he feels guilty. Good. He should.

I feel guilty too. But for a different reason. I knew what Uncle Mike was going through and didn't do anything. I can't believe I told him it was a good idea to come out to the family. I should have found a way to see him Friday night. Or even Saturday. I could tell he was in a weird mood after that phone call. If I'd gone to see him, maybe I would have figured out what he was planning. I could have talked him out of it. I should have at least called him back.

I don't cry at the funeral service. I don't cry at the burial. As I watch the casket being lowered into the ground, it's like I'm outside of my body. Like I'm not here at all.

CHAPTER
17

Days pass. Weeks pass. I go to school. Sit in my classes. Camp under the tree at lunch. I've stopped going into the cafeteria for food. The less chance of running into my ex-teammates the better. I don't like being reminded of what I'm missing. The Crusaders are in the playoffs. I'm happy for them, but … I'm not.

So, like today, I spend my lunch money at the vending machines. A bag of Fritos lands next to the Snickers bar I just bought. Lunch of champions. I grab my stash.

"Hey." Randi is standing behind me.

"Hey," I mutter back. I haven't seen her in a while. She looks healthy. Fit. Like most starters do after a full season. I looked like that a year ago. I didn't even glance in the mirror this morning.

She eyes my junk food. "That your lunch?"

"Yeah."

She nods. "So I just heard about your uncle. I wish I'd heard sooner. I'm … really sorry. I know you guys were close."

I shrug. I never know how to respond when people say, "I'm sorry." It's okay? Me too? Yeah whatever? So I've stopped saying anything.

She fidgets. Looks at the floor. Then looks at my face like there's a booger the size of a house on it and she doesn't know how to tell me. "Are you … okay?" she finally asks.

I stand there. The answer I'd tell my best friend: No, I'm not okay. I feel like crap every second of every single day. The answer I give to my former best friend: "Yeah. Getting by."

She nods again. "Okay. Just checking." Then she says, "Does your dad still have your phone?"

"Yeah."

"Oh. I was going to say you can call or text me if you want to."

"That's not gonna happen."

"Well, you know …." She shrugs. "When you get it back." She holds up her hand in a wave. Starts walking away. Stops and turns. "It's cool you were at the Solano game. Thanks for cheering. Tiana's pretty good but we could really use you in the playoffs." She leaves.

A week or two ago what she just said would have made

me feel something. Happy. Sad. Now it just passes through me like air.

I head outside to the tree. Inez and Clarence are already there. I set my lunch and backpack on the ground. Rummage around for my water bottle. Open it and take a long swig of vodka. It's two-thirds gone already. I was hoping it would last another day, but that's not likely. I offer it to Clarence.

"No thanks," he says. "My brother scored yesterday."

"And he shared?" I ask in disbelief. I hand the bottle to Inez. From what Clarence has told us, his brother is stingy with his weed.

He grins slyly. "Not shared, exactly." He licks his finger and holds it in the air, checking for a breeze. He looks around for teachers. The conditions must be right, because he lights his joint.

I'm pretty sure this is why Randi asked if I was okay— my new friends. If our roles were reversed, if it was Randi out here with All Saints druggies, I'd be worried about her. But Clarence and Inez aren't so bad. They're just misunderstood. Rejected. Coping. Like me. Exactly like me. I lean my back against the tree. Feel the buzz. Let it wash over me. Let it keep that room in my brain cozy and tight.

I get to work on time that afternoon. Except for that one Saturday, I'm always on time. I can't tell you why. I'm screwing up every other part of my life.

"Hi, Gabby." Jo is pushing a handcart.

"Hi." I ka-chunk my timecard.

"Can you help Evan at the loading dock? Veggie delivery."

I head over to the loading dock. Step into the truck. Heft a box of lettuce and carry it into the warehouse.

Evan passes me coming the other way. "Hi, Talks-a-lot."

I drop the box onto the pushcart. Evan's right behind me when I turn around. His arms are crossed.

"You okay?" he asks.

"God, what is going on today? Yeah, I'm fine. Why?"

"You didn't say hi."

"Well, sorry. Hi."

"And you're grumpy."

I roll my eyes.

He reaches out. Brushes a strand of hair off my cheek. Gives me a lopsided grin.

I smile. I can't help it. That grin gets to me.

"If you come to Jo's tonight, I promise I'll behave."

I take a deep breath. Evan and I still flirt at work. Kiss when we're sure Jake won't see us. But I haven't been to another one of their parties. The image of him and Jo groping each other will be forever seared on the back of my eyelids. They keep telling me it was just one of those things. You know, drugs, booze, silly hormones. But it was also the night Uncle Mike died. Maybe if I'd been home. Maybe, maybe, maybe.

I shake my head.

He cups his hand under my chin, whispers, "Dude, you are killing me. I want you."

"I'll try." It's the same thing I've been telling him every Friday and Saturday night. "Can you swipe me another bottle?" I ask. "The Stoli. With the blue label."

He sighs. "Yeah, sure."

I ride home with Mom. The bottle is in my backpack between my feet. We come to a corner. A guy steps into the crosswalk. Mom slows the car. The guy gets back on the curb. Waves us on. What would have happened if he hadn't seen us? If Mom hadn't seen him? Hadn't slowed down? If she'd hit him? Would he have died? Or been injured? Like, paralyzed? If you wanted to do it right, you'd need to step in front of something bigger. A truck. A semi-truck.

Then I'm thinking about Uncle Mike. I picture him tying the rope around a rafter in the garage. Making sure it was tight. Tying a noose. Kicking the upside-down bucket out from under him. How did he learn to do all that? On the Internet? Or did he figure it out himself? Did it hurt? I can't imagine choking to death. I hope the pain didn't last long.

I take a deep breath. Dig my fingernails into my palms. Stop it, I tell myself.

Stop it. Stop it.

I keep thinking about this stuff. I glance over at Mom.

She's been quiet since Uncle Mike died. Like the rest of the family. No one talks about it. We're all in our own little worlds. I wonder if they think about death as much as I do. If they get what I'm going through. I'd like to ask Mom. Ask her right now. But I'm sure she doesn't. She's never understood anything else about me. Only Uncle Mike understood. And he's dead. He left me to deal with this all by myself. I hate him for leaving me. And hating him makes me hate myself more than I already do.

CHAPTER

18

I sit on my bed that night, a textbook on my lap. I'm not reading it. I don't know which book it is. It's in case Mom or Dad come into my room. Midterm grades come out in a week. I wonder what they'll do when they find out my grades have gone down instead of up. I don't give a crap about my phone anymore. There's no one to call and no one to call me. I do care about being grounded, though. It's annoying. They still check my room, but it's down to about once a night. I don't know if it's because they're starting to trust me or they just don't care anymore.

I'm stressed about having to repeat the semester. School feels like a hill I'm supposed to climb. But it keeps raining and raining and the trail gets slicker and slicker. Every time I take a step, I slide backward, farther down than I was before.

I grip my water bottle. Take a sip. It still burns my throat a little, but I don't think about it. I think about what would happen if I drank the whole thing. The whole bottle Evan gave me today. It would probably kill me. I looked it up on the Internet after dinner. Alcohol poisoning. Depends on how big you are. How fast you drink. If you've eaten anything beforehand.

I bite my lip. Take a longer drink. I'm doing it again. Thinking about death. I force myself to look down at my book. My eyes have trouble focusing. The text swims. I can make out a painting of an old guy wearing a cape and a weird hat. He's standing up in a boat full of other men. Well, that's just stupid. He could tip the boat over. Everyone would drown.

I throw the book across my room.

Jump off my bed.

Look for Rosie. She's in the living room. Along with everyone else. Eyes glazed. Zombieland.

"Rosie, did you borrow my red hoodie?" I try to not slur, to sound like my normal, snarky self.

She drops her jaw. "No."

"Well, I can't find it. I'm about to search your room."

"Don't you dare!" She's on her feet, running to her room.

Once we're both there, I close her door.

She screams in my face, "I didn't borrow your stupid hoodie!"

"I know! I need you to do me a favor."

It's cold tonight. I rub my arms and walk faster. Picture my jacket hanging in the hall closet. Before I left the house, I told Rosie to turn on her side, away from the door. So Mom and Dad wouldn't see her face. It only took a couple of threats to get her to sleep in my bed. Marijuana. Boys. It wasn't a spur-of-the-moment idea. I figured it out a couple weeks ago. But tonight I have to get out of the house. Get my brain on other things.

I open the door to Jo's apartment. Same booming music. I see maybe one or two new faces, but otherwise it's the same. I wonder if partying ever gets boring. I step over people's legs. There's a bong underneath me.

"Hey," I murmur, holding out my hand.

A guy hands it up to me with the lighter. I take a long hit. In a few seconds the smoke gets where it belongs. The floor rolls under my feet. My brain floats … nice. Really nice.

I look toward the kitchen. There's Evan, behind the counter. My heart beats a little faster. My brain smiles. I think my mouth does too. God, I like Evan. Except Evan is with someone. The blonde woman from that first party.

She's nuzzling his neck. His arms are wrapped around her waist. I march into the kitchen. Scoot by them. Pour myself a tall shot of vodka. Down it.

I whisper in Evan's free ear, "Hey."

He turns. Looks at me. Grins. He says something to blondie. She shrugs, winks at him, and walks away. Now I'm in blondie's place. Now Evan's arms are around my waist.

"You made it." His hot breath makes my ear tingle. Then we're kissing. And my brain goes offline.

I'm in the bathroom, puking. When my stomach is empty, I lean back, wipe my mouth. My knees hurt from kneeling. I wonder how long I've been in here. Someone's pounding hard on the door. Dad? Where the hell am I? I hear music and talking. Jo's. I'm at Jo's.

"Will you hurry up?" someone yells.

I stagger to my feet. Flush the toilet. Rinse my mouth in the sink. Unlock the door and a girl rushes in, slamming the door behind her.

The last thing I remember is kissing Evan. In the kitchen. Evan. God, I like Evan. I really, really like Evan. I head to the kitchen. He's not there. Jo is getting a beer out of the fridge.

"Where's Evan?" I ask.

"Where you left him."

I squint.

She shakes her head. "You are so loaded." Then she says, "In the bedroom."

The bedroom. Okay. I think that's okay. Yeah, it is okay. This is why I came here tonight. To hook up with Evan. Get my mind on other things.

I turn for the hallway.

"Uh, just a warning," Jo says. "Since I know you're squeamish about this stuff. Becca got to him after you locked yourself in the bathroom."

What is she talking about? I walk down the hallway. The bedroom door is shut. I open it. Evan is on top of the blonde woman. They're doing it. They're having sex. I think about screaming. I think about walking in there. Pulling her out from under him. Punching her in the face. Kicking her. Scratching her.

Instead I close the door. Stuff the image of Evan and Becca into the room in my brain. Close that door too.

I stagger through the apartment toward the front door.

"Gabby, are you okay?" Jo calls from the kitchen.

Are you okay, are you okay, are you okay?

"He really likes you," she says. "But he likes a lot of people. That's just the way he is."

I walk home.

CHAPTER

19

I should be getting dressed for work. But I'm standing in front of my closet, staring at a cardboard box. Gabby is printed across the top with a Sharpie. Dad handed it to me after Uncle Mike's funeral. Abuelita found it in Uncle Mike's room. I set the box on the floor of my closet. That's where it still is, unopened.

I'm thinking about the last time I talked to Uncle Mike on the phone. He sounded okay. Happy, even. I don't get it. If he was happy, why did he hang himself? I consider opening the box, like I have a hundred times. Maybe there's a clue in there. But the fact he picked out stuff for me after he'd already decided to kill himself. I don't know. That's messed up. Not something I can deal with. I grab my shoes and close the closet. Fill up my water bottle and take it with me.

I just make the 7:40 bus. It's Saturday, so not crowded. I sit next to the window. My reflection stares back at me. For a second, I'm not sure who it is. The girl's hair is dull and clumped. Her makeup doesn't begin to cover the dark circles under her eyes. She's got lines at the corners of her mouth from frowning. Thank God the bus comes to my stop so I don't have to look at her anymore.

I walk to the warehouse on autopilot. I should have a plan for what I'll say to Evan. Can't think of one.

"Hey," he says when I walk in.

I do my timecard.

He's in his usual position holding up the wall. Gripping a coffee cup. Eyes closed. I take the opportunity to stare at him. Drink him in. The graceful way he moves the cup to his lips. Those beautiful lips. Why do I still like him? After last night the sight of him should make me sick.

But I still want him.

Jo said Evan likes a lot of people. That's just the way he is. I guess I don't see anything wrong with that. As long as I'm one of the people he likes. Because he makes me feel like I'm worth something. No one else in my life does that. Tony used to. Randi used to. Uncle Mike used to.

Evan swallows his coffee. Looks over at me and smiles.

I smile back.

"Sorry you left early," he says. "We were about to have a good time."

About to? The part I remember was good. Wasn't it?

"Jo said you blacked out."

Blacked out. Isn't that something that happens to hard-core addicts? "I don't know. I don't think so."

He pushes himself away from the wall. "Maybe you shouldn't drink so much."

I stare at him, sort of disbelieving what he's saying. "You drink. You even drink at work."

A look crosses his face. It makes my heart catch. Because it reminds me of my dad when he's disappointed in me.

"Yeah, I drink," he says, "but I've never blacked out. Never. I know what I'm doing." He crumples his coffee cup. "Get a grip, Talks-a-lot. Know your limits. It's the only way you can hold a job and have a life." He looks at the clock. "Jo is late again." He heads to Jake's office.

I watch him and I'm six years old. Running after Dad. Begging him to pick me up. Wanting him to be happy with me again. Don't hate me. Please don't hate me. I take a deep breath. Set my water bottle on the floor near the time clock. Slowly follow Evan to Jake's office.

While we're there, Jo calls in sick. We're slammed with deliveries. The store is running low on everything. Jake gets Hutch to come in on his day off. Evan spends most of his time at the loading dock. I'm in the store, stocking shelves. We don't see much of each other. I'm back in Zombieland, just doing my job. Not thinking.

By ten I'm feeling hyper. Antsy. A little shaky. On my way to break, I glance at my water bottle. Think of what Evan said. Leave it. Change my mind. Pick it up.

Evan is already at the picnic table, smoking. I sit next to him. Close enough so we're almost touching. Hope that whatever was bugging him earlier was just hangover pissiness. He likes me. I know he does. He pulls out his flask and takes a drink. Doesn't offer me any. Glances at my plastic bottle. Suddenly, I'm seeing it like he does. It's dented, the label is torn off. It's well used. Overused.

Evan sighs and sets his cigarette in an ashtray. Reaches into his pocket. Pulls out a plastic baggie and opens it. "Hold out your hand," he says.

"Why?"

"Just do it."

I open my palm. He drops a pill into it.

"Don't mix this with what's in your bottle," he says. "Try it alone sometime. Broaden your horizons. Forget booze for a while."

I stare at the white tablet.

He takes a drag on his cigarette. Blows the smoke out in a thin stream. "Jo told me to leave you alone. She said you're too young. You don't know what you're doing." He shrugs. "I thought you could handle it. But, as always, she's right. You're an amateur."

He gets up from the table. "Might want to brush your hair, Talks-a-lot. You're kind of a mess."

I watch him walk back into the warehouse. I grip the pill in my fist. Gather my hair in my other hand and pull it back. Take a long swig from my water bottle. Then another.

It seems like only seconds have passed when I hear, "Hey! Break was over ten minutes ago!" Hutch glares at me from the doorway.

I get up slowly from the table. Shove the pill in my pocket. Pick up my half-empty water bottle. Think of walking across the parking lot, getting on a bus, and going home. But I don't feel like sitting in my prison room with a box of stuff from my dead uncle. Then I remember today is the first day of basketball playoffs. I could go. Except I don't know where it is. I don't even know who they're playing.

That's sad. So sad I think I might cry. But I can't cry because I'm focused on my feet. Carefully putting one in front of the other, in a straight line so I don't fall on my face. Which I picture in my mind. The picture of me falling is so funny it makes me laugh. Which is weird, because I was sad just a second ago. Wasn't I?

CHAPTER

20

I'm in the household aisle inside the store. Craning my neck at the top shelf. Where the box of wax paper in my hand needs to go. I get on my toes, raise my arm. Lose my balance. Reach out as I stumble. Sweep boxes off a shelf. Fall on the floor.

A customer runs over. "Are you all right?"

I'm on my side. Push myself onto my hands.

"That was a bad tumble." She's an older woman. Gray hair. Looks worried.

"I'm okay."

"Are you sure? Do you need help?"

"No, I'm okay!" To prove it, I get on my knees. Grab a lower shelf. Pull myself up. Sway when I get to my feet. The store spins.

The woman is still watching me. Her eyes narrowed. I wish she'd stop staring.

"You're a little wobbly," she says. "Did you hit your head?"

"No. I'm fine." I let go of the shelf. Try to stand straight. Like a person who hasn't been drinking.

She nods. Returns to her shopping cart. Pushes it away.

I take a deep breath. Bend over and pick up the boxes of foil I knocked over. Throw them back where they belong. I glance up at the top shelf again. It's like Mount Everest. It's like, why do I give a crap?

"Cleanup in bulk foods," the intercom says.

Oh, cool. That's me. I leave the cart of wax paper in the middle of the aisle. When I get to bulk foods, it looks like the floor is covered with insects. Cockroaches. I shiver. Walk a little closer. No, they're almonds. Under the nut dispensers. Customers are stepping around them. I slowly drop to my hands and knees. Start picking them up one by one.

A guy wearing boots steps through them. Nuts crunch under his heels. Grind into the linoleum. He fills a plastic bag with peanuts.

I look up at him. "Hey, do you mind?"

He stares down at me, like I'm a cockroach. "Why don't you use a broom?" Now he laughs like I'm an idiot. When he's done with the peanuts, he walks back through the almonds again.

I stagger to my feet. "Jerk!"

He shakes his head. Flips me off. Keeps walking.

I'm shaking. Balling my fingers into fists. I start to follow him.

"Do you work here?"

I twist around. A woman is pushing a cart with a kid in it. He's swinging his legs. His feet hit the cart with a loud *choing-choing-choing*.

"Do you carry gluten-free bread?" she asks.

"What? I don't know."

Choing-choing-choing.

She rolls her eyes. "Well, if you did, where would it be?"

Choing-choing-choing.

I glare at her. "I don't have a damn clue!"

"Excuse me?"

Choing-choing-choing.

"I said damn clue. I don't have one."

Her eyes bug out. "I'm talking to the manager. What's your name?"

I hesitate. "Mary Smith." I head for the warehouse. Still shaking. Shove my way through the double doors. Walk straight to the time clock. Look for my water bottle. It's gone. I search around. Can't find it.

Evan.

I march to the loading dock. He's driving the forklift.

"Hey!" I yell. He doesn't hear me. I run ahead of him and step in front of Big Bird.

It lurches to a stop. "Jesus!" Evan screams. "What's wrong with you?"

"Where's my water bottle?"

He hesitates. "I don't know."

"Yes you do. *Where is it?*"

"I said I don't know. Get out of my way."

"Where is it?"

Hutch walks over. His arms crossed. "What's going on?"

"She's lost her water bottle," Evan says.

Hutch grabs me by the arm and pulls me out of Evan's way.

"Thanks," Evan says. He drives past us.

"Let go." I yank my arm back.

Hutch squints at me for several seconds. "You're drunk."

"I am not."

"Yeah?" He reaches into his pocket. Pulls something out. Shows me a bronze-colored coin. "Five years sober last month. I know a drunk."

I squint back at him. "Good for you. I just want my water bottle."

"Full of vodka, right?" His voice softens. "Go home and sober up. I'll tell Jake you got the stomach flu."

I didn't cry after Uncle Mike died. For two months I haven't cried. But now I feel tears pushing against my eyes.

My throat tightens. I whisper, "What if I don't want to sober up?"

Hutch sighs. "You may not think you do, but you do. Believe me. If you want to keep your job, go home. Right now."

I don't care about keeping my job. But I don't want to stay here, either. I stagger away. Head for the door. See my water bottle. It's where I left it. On the shelf next to the toilet paper. I grab it.

I drink what's left as I'm walking across the parking lot. Drop the empty bottle on the ground. Realize I forgot to do my timecard. Don't care.

When I get on the bus, it's hard to see the girl in the window. She's a blur. I think she's crying too. I hope she is. I mean, I don't like thinking anyone else is this miserable. But I want the company. So I'm not so friggin' lonely. A chicken in a pig pen. Or is it a pig in a chicken coop. Crap, Uncle Mike. Now I'll never know. Why did you kill yourself? I dig my fingernails into my knees. Dig harder and harder and harder.

When I get to my room, I open the closet. Reach behind my folded sweaters. Pull out the vodka bottle. It's two-thirds full. I hope it's enough.

I take the white tablet out of my pocket. Pop it in my mouth. Down it with a swig of vodka. Drink the rest of the bottle as fast as I can. I hardly ate anything for lunch.

There's nothing in my stomach to get in the alcohol's way. Which makes me wonder if I planned this. Maybe. When Evan gave me that pill, part of me knew it was my way out. My guarantee.

I should write a note while I can still move. I grab my notebook and a pen from my desk. Carry them with me to bed. I sit there. Nothing. I have nothing to say. To anyone. I just want this to be over with. I lie down.

As I rest my head on my pillow, I figure something out. About Uncle Mike. Why he was happy the last time we talked. It's because he knew all the crap in his life was about to end. He'd made up his mind what to do. He didn't have anything to worry about anymore. He was at peace.

I get it, Uncle Mike. I finally, totally get it.

CHAPTER

21

I hear people talking. Their voices are loud. Rushed. I think of opening my eyes. But my eyelids are too heavy. I'm so sleepy. Please stop talking. I want to sleep. Just let me sleep.

There's a hissing sound. And a *beep-beep-beep-beep*. I wish the noises would stop. It's annoying. I try to open my mouth. To tell the room to shut up. But I can't part my lips. It's like they're glued shut.

I'm in my backyard. Practicing the waltz for my *quinceañera*. I want the steps to be perfect. Cannot make an ass out of myself on my big birthday. I'm dancing with Tony. We twirl around and around. Feel so silly we start laughing. Fall into each other's arms.

Now I'm waltzing with my dad. We're surrounded by

friends and relatives. Randi is there. So is Celia. Uncle Mike. Everyone is smiling as us. At me. Dad's looking into my eyes. His smile is bigger than anyone's.

"Gabriella," Mom calls.

I stop dancing. What?

"Gabby!"

I open my eyes. The light is bright. It hurts. I close them.

"Gabby, *por favor*, stay awake!"

I open my eyes again. Squint into the light. Turn my head. Mom's face is inches from mine. She looks so worried. Now she's crying. No, Mom, don't cry. She's petting my head. Squeezing my hand. I squeeze back. It's okay, Mom. Whatever is wrong, it's okay.

I wake up. It's dark. Night? My head hurts. A lot. There's a little light in the room. Coming from the doorway. I'm not lying flat. My back is raised. I remember seeing Mom a while ago. Did she prop pillows behind me? Then I hear a beeping sound. A hiss of air. There's something in my nose! I reach up to touch it. But there's a painful tug on my arm. I reach with my other hand. There's a tube attached to my wrist. And a tube in my nose!

I start to panic. The beeping goes faster. I hear rustling nearby.

"Gabby?" It's Dad. He stands over me. His forehead is creased with worry.

"What's wrong! Where am I?"

"You're in a hospital. You ...." He doesn't finish. He starts crying.

I what? Why is Dad crying? Then I remember. I tried to kill myself. I drank vodka and took a pill. It didn't work. My emotions crash into each other. Regret. I so wanted it to work. Embarrassment. Mom and Dad must hate me for doing this. But they seem sad. And that makes me sad.

Mostly, I'm tired. I am just. So. Tired. I cannot deal with any of this right now.

"I need to sleep some more," I whisper.

Dad nods. Kisses my forehead. One of his tears drop on my cheek.

Gradually, I stay awake for longer amounts of time. Find out what happened. Saturday afternoon Rosie heard me puking. She found me choking on my own vomit. She turned me onto my side. Marta called 911. Dr. Su says the pill Evan gave me was a high-dosage pain killer. Combined with the alcohol, it did a number on my body. I had seizures. I was pretty much unconscious for a full day.

"You're lucky to be alive," Dr. Su tells me Sunday night. I don't know how to respond. So I don't.

I stay in the hospital Monday and Tuesday. They want to monitor me through detox. Make sure there's no brain damage. Flowers arrive. The card says, "Get well soon, Gabby!—the Crusaders." I know they're either from Randi or Coach Matthews.

A parade of people file in and out of my hospital room. Sometimes I'm asleep and Mom and Dad tell me later who stopped by. Rosie and Marta come in the afternoons after school. Abuelita visits. So do a couple of my uncles and aunts. Celia drives up from college. She's her usual high-pressure self, but she seems truly worried about me.

It amazes me how no one talks about what happened. Only the doctors and nurses use the words suicide and alcohol poisoning and addiction and depression. For my family it's like I'm here to have my tonsils removed. In a way, that's okay. I get it. They're ashamed. Suicide is a sin. Suicide says something bad about the whole family. That they failed because I failed. But it feels like everyone is throwing a bright, flowery blanket over me to hide my ugliness. They aren't seeing me. They aren't seeing what's really wrong.

I guess Tony was here while I slept. I'm glad no one woke me. I'm not sure how I feel about him. I'd rather see him when my head is a little straighter.

My biggest surprise visitor is Hutch. He lumbers in on Tuesday night. Mom knows him from the store. But Dad does a double take. Maybe it's the ponytail and snake tattoo.

"I'm glad you're okay," Hutch tells me. "If I knew you

were suicidal. I would have stayed with you on Saturday. I'm sorry."

His honesty is a relief. I notice Dad frown and squirm in his chair. "That's okay," I tell Hutch. "You didn't know."

He nods. "If you want to give AA a try sometime, call me at the warehouse."

"Sure." I want to ask about Evan. About Jo. If they know what happened. If they've asked about me. But I don't want to talk about them in front of my parents. So I say, "Has Jake hired someone to replace me?" Mom called Jake on Monday and told him I wouldn't be coming back to work. It looks like I'll be starting drug rehab after school. And I have homework to make up.

Hutch nods. "A buddy of mine."

"So not another little girl."

He smiles. "Nope." Squeezes my shoulder. "See you around."

Dr. Su checks me out of the hospital Wednesday morning. He gives me a prescription for antidepressants. "You're lucky to be alive," he tells me for like the hundredth time.

Right.

I've decided that hospitals suck. I'm glad to be leaving. But I'm not so sure about going home. Mom and Dad won't be so nice once their relief has worn off. I'm still failing school. I'm not any smarter than I used to be. Or a better student. My only friends at school are druggies. The guy I thought liked me thinks I'm worthless. My uncle is still dead. In other words, nothing has really changed.

And that worries the crap out of me.

CHAPTER

22

I won't go back to school until Monday. But I start therapy and rehab Thursday, the day after I get home from the hospital. Talk to strangers about my life? About drinking? I'd rather take ten geometry tests in a row. But I don't have a choice. Mom takes the rest of the week off so I won't be alone. Doctor's orders. She drives me to the therapist's office.

One of the first things Dr. Wiser asks me is, "How does it feel to be alive?"

Wow. I thought maybe we'd start off chatting about the weather. I think about her question. "I don't know. Fine, I guess."

"All right." She smiles. "What's fine about it?"

I guess I won't be hiding under a flowery blanket in here. I feel uncomfortable sitting here. It's not like I imagined. Dr. Wiser doesn't accept one-word answers.

Come to find out. I'm depressed. Maybe I have been for a long time. A few years, even. That might be where my anger comes from. The fights in basketball. Getting aggressive when I'm upset. Those are symptoms of depression, which is news to me. Depression might even run in my family, like diabetes or heart disease.

Wiser says when all of my problems heaped up on me they just made my depression worse. Then Uncle Mike committed suicide. The grief sent me into a tailspin. I coped by getting drunk. His death also planted a seed in my brain. Like, if my favorite uncle solved all his problems by killing himself, then I could do the same thing.

The counseling session ends. My brain hurts. It's on overload. But at least it's information I can use. I have a disease. It can be helped with medication and counseling. Lots of people are going through the same thing as me. So I'm weird … but normal. Normally weird, I guess. I walk out of her office feeling a little less crazy than when I walked in.

I have a couple hours to process all of Dr. Wiser's juicy information. Then I go to rehab. It's held in a church basement. There are ten other kids around my age and an adult counselor sitting in a circle. It's an ongoing group, which means I'm the newcomer. Fun. I sit quietly with my arms crossed.

They start talking about triggers. Whoa, as in guns?

But I quickly figure it out. Triggers are things that make you want to drink or use drugs again. One girl, Bianca, says "I have a hard time going to movies. I used to smoke weed first."

The counselor, Alan, looks at me. "What about you, Gabby? What's your biggest trigger?"

Now everyone's staring at me.

Great. I was hoping I wouldn't have to talk my first time. But I'll feel like a total dickwad if I don't say something. I clear my throat. "Um … my bedroom. And a tree at school. I drink there. Did drink there. At lunch." I'm so embarrassed I want to crawl under my chair.

But a couple of kids are nodding. One of them, I don't remember his name, says, "I can't go near half the trees on campus. The craving for meth kills me."

Come to find out I have to avoid triggers. Really? Are you friggin' kidding me? I raise my hand.

"Yes, Gabby?" Alan says. "You can just speak up. You don't need to raise your hand."

"Okay. What about my room? I can't avoid my bedroom. I sleep in there."

Kids laugh. What jerks.

But then Alan says, "How many of you have your bedroom as a trigger?"

Every person raises their hand.

Oh.

Alan says, "Give Gabby a few ideas for handling cravings when she's in her bedroom."

They do. Some of the ideas sound stupid. But I guess I can at least try.

The next night, Friday, there's a knock on my door. Two quick taps, then a third tap. Tony.

I take a deep breath. Open the door. "Hey."

"Hey," he says. I haven't seen him in weeks. He looks exactly the same. Exactly. God, I love Tony. He's so … familiar.

"How's it going?" His voice is soft. Tentative. Like I might break if he says the wrong thing.

"I'm tired. But better than I was a week ago."

He nods. "That's good. I'm really glad you didn't. …"

I wait, but he can't seem to get the words out. "Successfully kill myself?" I finish for him.

He cringes. Nods.

"Why don't we sit in the backyard," I say. "The rubber band's not doing such a great job."

He raises an eyebrow.

I hold up my wrist. Show him the thick rubber band around it. Snap it. "The pain is supposed to distract me from drinking."

"Oh. Very high tech."

We walk into the backyard and sit on the swings. I push

myself back and forth with my toes. It's a nice March night. Just the right temperature. I'm glad I never drank out here. I'd hate to have to avoid the yard.

Tony stares at the ground. "I'm sorry," he finally says. "I should have been around for you more. Especially after your uncle. …"

I roll my eyes. "Committed suicide?"

He nods.

I think about it. Having a friend, any friend, might have helped. But I didn't give him a chance. "You would have helped if I'd asked, right?"

"Of course."

"Then don't feel guilty for not knowing."

He pauses. Grips the chains. "Gabby, I … need to tell you something. I know the timing sucks. But I want you to find out from me. Not some other way."

I stop my swing and stare at him.

"I'm dating someone. A girl from school."

I close my eyes. Lean my head against the chains. I agreed all those weeks ago we should break up. It was the right decision. It's still the right decision. I have to be okay with this. I have to. But it doesn't feel so good.

"I'm sorry," he says.

I get up from the swing.

Tony stands too. He faces me and takes my hands. "I love you, Gabby. I will always love you. But—"

"We're not right for each other."

He hesitates. Nods. "But I'm your friend. I'm here for you. Okay?"

I don't respond.

"Okay?" He grips my hands tighter.

"Yeah, okay!" I pull my hands away.

"Now I feel like crap," he says.

"You should." Then I see the fear and guilt in his eyes. "Don't worry. I'm not going to kill myself over you."

He bites his lip.

"Really. I have new coping skills." I snap the rubber band on my wrist.

He smiles. We share a long look. He kisses my cheek. And leaves.

CHAPTER

23

After Tony leaves, I want to get drunk. Badly. I have never in my life wanted a drink so much. So I listen to music. Tell myself the cravings will pass. Try some other stupid tricks I learned in rehab. Like thinking about the positives of not drinking (graduating high school, for example). Reminding myself of a goal that will get messed up if I drink again. Except, I don't have a goal. I don't have one friggin' goal.

Mom and Dad were smart to get rid of all the alcohol in the house. Because around midnight I go searching. Refrigerator. Cupboards. I even look in the garage. They've cleaned everything out. I hate this feeling of being out of control. Of hating my life. By the time I get to the bathroom, I'm shaking. I look above the sink for painkillers. Cold meds. Anything. But there's not even an aspirin bottle.

The bathroom door opens. Mom's eyes widen when she sees me searching through the medicine cabinet. But she doesn't yell. Doesn't say anything. She walks over. Wraps her arms around me. Whispers, "Gabriella. Please don't hurt yourself again. I would never forgive myself. *Te quiero*. I love you so much."

I hug her back. "I love you too." Then I'm crying. Really crying. She leads me back to my bedroom. Sits with me until I fall sleep.

The rest of the weekend sucks as much as Friday. Especially Saturday. I think about work. About Evan. About drinking and partying. Mom gets Dad to return my phone so I can call Dr. Wiser or Alan, the rehab counselor, if I need to. Dad doesn't complain. I guess even he sees what a mess I am.

Monday rolls around and I'm still alive. I haven't had a drink. I'm sick of being home. But I've got very mixed feelings about going to school. I'm a seventeen-year-old drunk who almost killed herself. I can't imagine the gossip that's been traveling around campus. And then there's lunch. I can't go back to the tree with Clarence and Inez. I'll relapse for sure.

I start down the main hallway. Feel like I've got a disease they're afraid of catching. Kids stare. There's a hiss of whispers. I lower my eyes. God, I wish I had my water bottle. I can feel the shakes coming on.

"Hey, Gabby." I look up. It's Randi, walking next to me.

"Hey."

"Want some company to your locker?"

"Yeah. Please." Thank you. Thank you. I already feel kids going back to whatever they were doing. Like I'm not as contagious anymore.

"So how are you feeling?" Randi asks.

"Crappy."

"I can't imagine what you're going through."

I'm so sick of talking about me. "How are the playoffs?"

"Oh. We lost in the first round."

"No way."

"Yeah." She adjusts her backpack on her shoulder. "We tanked. Tiana choked under the pressure. Can't blame it all on her, of course, but. …" She shrugs.

We've reached my locker. As I turn the combination lock, I remember loving the pressure of playoffs. I always played my best when it meant the most.

"I was talking to Coach last Monday," Randi says. "When we were arranging sending flowers to the hospital. She said she wished you were still on the team. You're the best small forward she's ever coached."

I grab stuff out of my locker. Slam the door closed.

"I thought you should know," she says.

I nod.

"So are you still grounded?"

I think about it. "Probably. My grades still suck." I pat my backpack. "Got my phone, though."

Randi smiles. "Cool." She looks down the hallway. "Guess I'd better go." She glances at me. "I'm really glad you're okay."

"Thanks."

"I'll hold a spot for you at lunch. If you want."

I'm not sure that's what I want. I don't know if I'm ready to hang out with the team. "Maybe."

She nods and heads to English.

As I walk to social studies I notice my steps are a little lighter. I'm holding my head a little higher. I sit at my desk. Quickly grab my phone. Send Randi a text before class starts. "Thx for the flowers. And for walking with me. See you at lunch."

The next time I go to Dr. Wiser, she says it will take several weeks for the meds to kick in. And she might have to switch me to another brand if these don't work. It's a pain. I just want to feel better.

During those weeks I go to rehab. Go to therapy. Mom and Dad go too. Sometimes just the two of them see Dr. Wiser. Sometimes they go with me. It's hard for them. They can't wrap their heads around our family having mental health problems. That it's not my fault or someone else's fault. So things are not all rosy. They still expect a lot out of me, especially Dad. But they seem to be figuring out I'm not Celia. That getting a few Cs is not a crime. And that basketball is just as good a way to get into college as straight As.

The thought of suicide is always there. Like a huge hairy animal with its claws dug deep into my back. That's when I talk to Mom. Or call Dr. Wiser or Alan. I even call Hutch when no one else is around. I try not to call Randi and Tony too much. At least not when I'm feeling like crap. They're my friends. I don't want to burn them out.

I'm standing in front of my closet, looking for my team jacket. It's May. We're having a big end-of-school assembly tomorrow. Coach Matthews wants me to sit with the rest of the team. I'm feeling a little happier. The meds are finally working. The cravings for alcohol are still there. But not as bad. My grades aren't wonderful, but I'm passing.

I find my jacket on the floor. Next to the box from Uncle Mike. I grab the jacket and ignore the box like I always do. I'm about to turn away but notice something. The room in my brain. The one where I used to store stuff I didn't want to think about. I thought it was empty—of Tony, Randi, basketball, my grades, my parents, Evan. But it's not. A box is jammed tight into the corner.

This box. Uncle Mike's box.

I drag it out of the closet. Into the middle of my

bedroom. Press my hands on the top. Wonder if I'm ready. Take a deep breath and open it.

There's not a lot in there. A teddy bear we won together at the county fair. I insisted he keep it. A silly button from his bulletin board that says, Don't Worry, Be Happy. A newspaper article about my basketball team. It's like I'm in Uncle Mike's room again. Talking. Laughing. About anything. Everything. Feeling like I belong. That we both belong.

The last thing in the box is a framed photo. I carry it to my dresser. Set it under my portrait. It's of Uncle Mike and me at my *quinceañera*. Me in my sparkly tiara, the queen of unicorns. Standing with my favorite uncle in the world.

WANT TO KEEP READING?

Turn the page for a sneak peek at another book from the Gravel Road series: M.G. Higgins's *I'm Just Me*.

ISBN: 978-1-62250-721-4

CHAPTER 1

Nasreen

I knock on my brother's door. His rap music is so loud, I'm sure he can't hear me. I pound louder. "Jaffar! Open up!"

The volume goes down. He opens his door a crack and glares at me. "What?"

I clear my throat. He never lets me forget that he's older than me. That I'm just his little sister. "I need your help," I say.

He glances at the pamphlets I'm holding. "College brochures? You're only a junior."

"I know. I'm starting early."

He rolls his eyes. "Of course you are."

"I don't have a clue where to go or how to apply."

"Okay." He sighs. "Come in." He takes the pamphlets from me. Shakes his head as he glances at the first cover. "Harvard? No way."

"Why not?"

He fingers through the rest. "Cal Tech? MIT? Stanford? Nasreen, these are all top universities."

"So?"

"So our parents aren't rich."

"Mr. Clarke said I can apply for scholarships."

"I applied for scholarships and where am I going?"

"But you want to be an accountant. State college is perfect for you."

"Oh, that's right," he says. "You're the brains in the family." He shoves the brochures back at me.

"I just want your advice."

"And who advised me? No one. Because I'm the oldest and did it myself. Go online and figure it out." He turns his music up.

I leave, closing the door behind me.

Back in my bedroom, I set the brochures on my desk. I think about asking my parents. But they know nothing about American colleges. As I sink into my beanbag chair, I imagine all the kids at school whose parents will be helping them decide which colleges to apply to. Parents who aren't from Pakistan and get confused by American rules and language.

Taking a deep breath, I pull my calculus book onto my lap. I enter a few numbers into my graphing calculator and try to ignore Jaffar's loud music thumping through our shared wall.

By ten o'clock, my homework is finished. I wish I had

more. I start thinking about school tomorrow. The familiar knot ties in my stomach.

Mom pokes her head around my door. "It's time for bed, Nasreen," she says in Punjabi.

"I know," I mutter back in English.

"What's wrong?"

"Nothing."

She stares at me a moment. Then she says, "Good night," closing my door.

My parents have a hard enough time just getting by in this country. I decided a long time ago I wouldn't be one of the things they had to worry about. Just a year and a half. A year and a half and I won't have to deal with the students at Arondale High School anymore.

It's a little too early when I get to the bus stop. I lean against a tree, away from the others, trying to make myself invisible. When the bus pulls up, I stand at the back of the crowd, my jaw tight, my eyes lowered. Guys jostle and shove each other as they get on.

We're one of the first stops. That's good because I can always find an empty seat. Not so good because it's twenty more minutes until we get to school.

The bus starts moving. From the back seat, Samantha shouts, "Hey, I just figured out why she wears that stupid scarf!"

"Why?" her friend Melody asks, setting her up.

"To protect her head from bird poop. I wish *I* had one."

They laugh.

The bus driver glares at them in the rearview mirror and shakes her head. Samantha and her friends won't say anything else, or they'll get written up. I shrink into my seat anyway. At the next stop, Kyle Spencer sits behind me. My shoulders rise protectively around my neck.

"Hi, Nasty Nasreen," he whispers through my *hijab*. I lean away from him, curling my fingers into fists. I review math equations in my head.

At the next stop, someone sits next to me. No one *ever* shares my seat. Great. What do I have to put up with now?

ABOUT THE AUTHOR

M.G. Higgins writes fiction and nonfiction for children and young adults.

Her novel *Bi-Normal* won the 2013 Independent Publisher (IPPY) silver medal for Young Adult Fiction. Her novel *Falling Out of Place* was a 2013 Next Generation Indie Book Awards finalist and a 2014 Young Adult Library Services Association (YALSA) Quick Pick nominee. Her novel *I'm Just Me* won the 2014 IPPY silver medal for Multicultural Fiction—Juvenile/Young Adult. It was also a YALSA Quick Pick nominee.

Ms. Higgins's nearly thirty nonfiction titles range from science and technology to history and biographies. While her wide range of topics reflects her varied interests, she especially enjoys writing about mental health issues.

Before becoming a full-time writer, she worked as a school counselor and had a private counseling practice.

When she's not writing, Ms. Higgins enjoys hiking and taking photographs in the Arizona desert where she lives with her husband.